BlackHearts

The Witch Hunt

Christian Gaughf

free Rein publishing

BLACKHEARTS
The Witch Hunt

A FreeRein Publishing Book / published by arrangement
with the author

ISBN -13: 978-153-028118-3

FreeRein Publishing, Ontario, Canada
www.freereinpublishing.com

I dedicate this book to my editor, 'SMFP', and to my father.
Both who always believed in me and
never gave up on me.

I remember seeing color once in my life. It's been so long, that I forget them. I forget their names, what they look like, what objects were a particular color. I only remember that I once saw a difference in them. I remember feeling different as I looked upon them. But along with the color, I forget the feelings they gave me.

I don't feel anything now. All I see now is white, black and many shades gray. These are the only colors I see now. All the rest of them are lost to me. I do not understand them. They are no longer a concept I can just believe anymore. They are all gone.

1

All except one.

Blood.

I still see the crimson glow of blood. Its glow fascinates me as it mixes and blends into the world around it, giving it color as it consumes everything it touches. Turning the land into a canvas of bodies left in their final memories. So peaceful. So calm. Unlike the black before my eyes now.

I had lost count of them.

The Hidden. All soaring above me as I lay against the ashy rock. They were waiting for their chance to tear me apart. It was a shame for them that the chance would never come. They will continue to wait, nevertheless. They are hungry. Given enough time, the beasts will resort to eating each other. I always found myself staring as they ripped each other apart. They are creatures of instinct.

Just like me.

The plateau I was lying upon had a particularly

large nest of Lurkers. All of the towns and cities had been picked clean of humans and their like decades ago by these insatiable beasts. I was likely the first non-Hidden creature they had seen in a long time.

The Hidden always fascinated me. Especially the Lurkers with their black wings dancing in the dark skies, it seems as if the clouds were alive. They remind me a lot of humans. If you wound one, the rest will take advantage and eat it alive. It's ironic that the scream it evolved to make to let the others know of danger becomes the very thing that quickens its own death.

I was getting bored listening to the lightning and the repetitious screeching of the Lurkers. I was getting tired of waiting for them to attack one another. It was time to move on. Azathoth and Sothoth were getting bored as well. It felt so long ago that I used them last—so long since I pulled their triggers, and heard their songs. I think it's time to let the blood of the shadowed skies rain down.

I only needed one shot. I took some time to decide which one to use. So much alike, but so different at the same time. Both guns shined with silver, black handles, and thick, long barrels. Both imbued with markings of the past. The two chrome twins were my loyal companions in this world. They've killed many for me. Too many to count.

Ahh, Azathoth. My special girl. My right hand. She's made many more kills than Sothoth. She's a reliable one. Never let me down, or allowed another to touch her. She was different from Sothoth by the cross that hangs from her handle. Her songs weren't as lavish as her brother's but rarely does my prey need such extravagant music to die. Her thick, beautiful body always gave my prey the look of fear that I always enjoyed.

And of course, let's not forget you, Sothoth. Not as fast as his sister, but comes with the force of lightning and fire when the time comes. He can be a bit clumsy, but good for killing many in one shot. Unfortunately for you,

4

Sothoth, I only want to wound the creature. Not to send it back to the ashes. Azathoth it is.

I pulled Azathoth from her holster. Sorry to wake you, but the time has come. I took aim just above me, and pulled back on her hammer. I pulled the trigger and, like always, she did not disappoint. With as many lurkers as there were, it wasn't hard to hit one, but Azathoth knew right where to hit it.

Her bullet pierced the creature's neck. Much of its blood graced me with its caress as it fell. It wasn't long before the rest took notice. Before it even touched the giant rock, several of its brethren were already setting upon it. It only lasts a few seconds, but the feedings always look as if the sky, itself is devouring its prey.

There wasn't much left of the lurker after the rest were done feeding; a blackened husk of bone and entrails, but they left just enough for me to get what I needed. I took my pouch and scooped what remained of its black blood inside. This will be enough for what I need.

I took a moment to look out into the horizon for a moment as I stood at the edge. I picked the tallest plateau just for that. I could see a large city off to the east. Its giant towers of artificial concrete were clear to see from this high up. Likely a ghost town from the lack of light radiating from the structures, but there are always things to scavenge.

I held my arms out like wings to mock the Lurkers before I leaped. I could feel the cold air blowing past me as I plummeted. I closed my eyes for a second, listening to the continued thunder rolling and dropped out of the sky. I could feel myself falling faster as the wind pressed against my body.

It's times like this I wish I had wings.

As I reached the ground, I let my feet take the lead and let the wind take my body. As it did, I could feel the force of the fall weaken. My clothes and hair took to the wind as I neared the ground. My poncho, shirt, and equipment rising from me as the wind tried to take them. I was finally close enough to the ground to drop. The wind released and my feet finally touched the dead earth. The fall caused me to drop to one knee. I stood up, and dusted the ash from my clothing. A tiny puff of black smoke rising from the bandages of my right arm.

I'll make my way to the towers in the east. Maybe I can find what else I'm looking for there. If not, there is always something of use in dead cities.

The wind was calmer than normal here. The ash and dust barely lifted from the cracked earth. I was finally far enough away from the natural towers of stone and rock that they began to descend into the horizon. The city was in clear view from above, but nowhere in sight from where I was now. I knew I was going in the right direction. I just had to find the power source. That would lead me straight to the unnatural towers.

The Lurkers were still following me. I could hear them pass through the wind as they flew by. They will track me till I'm dead. It was unfortunate for them that my flesh would have to rot away before they could have me. I could not see them as they blended with the clouds. A black, angry sky that seemed to go on for eternity. It was the perfect home for The Hidden. It was a perfect hunting ground. For both them and me.

I could tell I was getting close to the power source as fewer Lurkers were around. I just had to keep my eye out for any light, and finding light here was not hard. The Hidden fear it. It is alien to them. They can't even tolerate the sight of it. They understand it as much as humans understand the darkness. They do not understand it, like I do.

I could see something before me. Something large, black, and motionless. As I got closer to it, I could begin making out details. It was buried in the ground, many long tendril like appendages rose from the base. I kept walking towards it until I could make out what it was. My first guess was the corpse of a Hidden, but alas, it was a large tree. The tree was leaned over as if a giant, deformed hand was clawing from underneath the ground, struggling to get out. How odd that it was hunched over all by itself. It was the only landmark for miles. *Why not take a look*, I thought to myself. I somehow felt a connection with this tree—as if it spoke to me

I inspected the tree as I approached it. It had been dead for a very long time. To even still call it a tree seemed wrong. The wood was black, petrified, to the point that it no longer gave way to the elements. Its branches curled like the fingers of a Hidden. I wasn't sure if the dried earth or the wind killed it first. Didn't matter. Just reminded me that the winds, the Gods, would eventually come back. If I was to avoid the same fate as this tree, I would need to seek shelter before the Gods returned and looked upon my intrusion with disdain.

The lurkers above began to dissipate over crossing many miles. I could see why. I had found what I was looking for. A light beaming from the ground some ways off in the distance. I was told this light is blue, but I do not understand that word. I made my way towards it. It wasn't hard to find light in the darkness. The light has a way of beckoning you when everything else is shadow.

There it was. The light led me to the veins of the city. A large, snake-like wire buried into the land, often arching up from the ground to expose its illuminated insides. All of the human cities share the same blood, and these giant, black veins bring life to them. Humans who travel the lands use these power sources as a means to keep the Hidden away. I use them to find my way to population when I needed supplies. Or when I'm just bored. Humans are always entertaining to me. It was likely I would find none there, however.

Looking in the direction the power vein seemed to be going, I could already see the next arch rising from the ground. It wasn't far, not quite a mile away. I headed north in the direction that the power supply guided me to. I knew it would lead me to the city I saw before. It was likely a town only populated by the dead, but the dead don't seem to care when you take things from them.

After many hours and many miles, I had reached the last arch before the city. Even this far, the buildings reached so far into the sky, the tops of them were essentially invisible. Blending into the darkness, only revealing themselves when lightning struck. There were no lights ahead, which meant its former inhabitants had succumbed to The Hidden. All it takes is a few minutes without light and an entire population can be overrun and eaten.

After miles and miles of cracked earth, I could finally see visible roads of black stone surrounded by buildings left derelict, decayed, and destroyed. Further I could see the chasm that bordered the main of the city, and the concrete bridge that connected it. The bridge looked oddly intact. It looked safe to cross. I made my way into the bulk of the ruin.

The main of the city was built of bleak, gray concrete and steel that may have once held glass but had long since been destroyed. From the ground, to the clouds, it was constructed of the same, cold rock. Tall structures of ash and dust conquered the sky. I suppose this was the humans' way of mocking the Gods of this land. Little good it did them in the end.

Abandoned mounts, once used for travel, had rusted and fused with the land. All just decoration of a time once before. There were hardly any remains of the humans apart from a few skulls, and a bone or two overlooked by the Lurkers. Lurkers… They're like that. They devour everything. Flesh, bone, it doesn't matter to them.

I began searching through the structures. The towers the humans made have begun to mimic the ground of this land—cracked, embraced by the ash of those who once inhabited it. They were old. Built hundreds of years ago, and left to rot for maybe only fifty or so. Some had already fallen. Cut down by the Gods they were designed to mock.

I continued searching through the concrete husks. Each one filled with the same stale scent of ash and burned metal. Each corridor the same as the last. There was evidence on the walls that I was not the first living, sentient being to visit this place recently.

The tattoos, the messages they left here, all varied in time, appearance, and the tools used to make them. Many of the markings said nothing at all. Just symbols and designs I couldn't understand. Others were markings left by travelers to warn others of potential danger. Some were written in paint, some were burned into the walls. Others were carved into the foundation, and some were written in blood—I had no time to look at them all. I was too focused on my own blood messages, but many stood out to me.

'No Hope.'

'Beware.'

'All Dead.'

'Welcome to the City of Torsos.'

I needed a piece of metal that I could hold in my hand.

Something thin enough that would heat quickly. While I

found lots of rebar and rusted sheets that flaked at mere

touch, I could not find anything like what I needed. But I

just had to keep looking. There must be something in one

of these structures that will work.

I finally found it. After sifting through the ashes

of virtually every husk, I finally found what I was looking

for. While searching through the debris, I saw it in the

hands of some skeletal remains in what looked to be an

old canteen. It was a knife. Bigger than what I needed, but it wasn't rusted, and it had a sharp point. It would work perfectly for what I needed.

I could almost smell the memories of this place. The scent of sharp liquor and the faint, putrid smell of sweat and body odor. Blood stains from even before The Hidden. A nest for the despaired and forgotten. The place gave off an aura I was familiar with. I felt at home here. The combination of desperation and hopelessness that filled the air was as strong as the scent of ash and decay.

This wasn't the first time I had been in one of these places. Not a bad place to make myself home for a few days as I searched the ruins. I found myself drawn to these homes of sin and violence. The smell of smoke and bottom-shelf poisons they called whiskey always reminded me of when William took me to places like this. A memory I found myself reliving often.

Deeper inside the canteen was the latrine in a

worse state of decay than the rest due to extreme water damage. The concrete walls cascaded with grime and mold. The floors were still coated with a thin layer of water, blood, and human waste. The light above hanging by a single, meager wire. Oddly, the wires were still alive, which flickered every minute or so, revealing the putrescence inside for very brief moments.

I decided to relieve myself while I was there. William always frowned when I did it anywhere else. I stood over one of the toilets as I urinated—despite there being little of it left. The metal it was made of had been torn and dented. It was difficult to say whether this was done during the attack or before it. After I was done, I shook it off, and looked around the room. I looked at where the sinks once were. Most of the mirrors were broken, except for one.

I wiped the thick layer of ash and grime off the mirror and was met with a familiar face. The face of a young man barely out of boyhood. White, frizzy hair. Gray, dead eyes that slanted slightly on the edges. A slender chin, jaw and nose. Skinny neck connected to a slender body, covered in black clothing and leather armor.

I looked down at myself. Everything on me was riddled with ash—the scarf around my neck, the tattered cloth poncho around my body that covered a fishnet shirt, the straps that held my equipment, and nearly a mile of wrapping that carried on to my right arm. A single leather, reinforced, fingerless glove on my left hand.

I looked down to my hip—Azathoth and Sothoth were resting to the right of me in their leather holsters. Satchels and small bags connected to my belt. Strong leather pants, along with matching boots with reinforced plating on the toes. All but the wrapping around me was black—camouflage for this land.

I looked up and smiled. He smiled back. I never thought I looked human enough when I smiled. I think people can tell when expressions are empty. William always told me to practice. Humans seem to know if something is off. My smile seemed to make others feel scared. He tried to teach me how to hide in plain sight, but I'm still learning.

I left the latrine and scrounged what could burn from the building. Wood was scarce in this city, so mounds of alcohol had to do. I poured several bottles into a rusted barrel just outside my new temporary home. I held my hand out as the black smoke rose from my arm and I felt the heat as my hand awakened the flame. This was probably the first flame this city has seen in a very long time.

I put my new knife through a small hole in the side of the can and into the flame as I unwrapped my arm. The lower layer of the wraps were already stained black. It had been so long since I changed them. The outside of the wraps were stained with dust, dirt, and

21

blood, whereas the side touching my skin had the smoldering aura of magic. It smelled of burned flesh and hair. Scents I am very fond of.

Ah, I could see them now—my prizes, my messages to the world. I had many of them. My entire right arm and some parts of my chest and back were covered in tattoos, as well as both palms of my hands. But they were not enough, I needed more. But for now, I just needed to touch up a few that had started to heal.

I pulled the knife from the fire. The blade now glowed as hot as the flame. It was ready. I grabbed the knife and sat down on the floor with my back to the wall, then took the pouch I used to obtain the Hidden blood, and laid it down beside me. I dipped the tip of the knife into the blood. The blade steamed and hissed as it touched the black poison.

The pain annoyed me as the hot knife burned my flesh. My body shook and my nerves convulsed as I dug it into the faded areas of my markings. I delicately traced them, making sure not to change a single letter, not a single word, not a single symbol. It was difficult to do it myself. I did not know most of them by heart, but I had burned them deeply last time, so there was no need. Just had to make sure the knife stayed steady. I dug into my flesh for what seemed like hours.

There wasn't a lot of blood after I had finished. The heat cauterized the site as I sank the knife in. There was almost none of my own blood on the ash. There was likely more of the Hidden blood on the ground than there was of mine, although it was hard to tell the difference between Hidden blood and my own. I dropped the knife as my arm went limp and my body grew weak as the poison began to take effect. The veins under my skin were already turning black. I would be the puppet to the blood for a while.

My body was already trying to pass out. I needed

to stay awake, so I fought one poison off with another. I didn't use all the bottles to start the fire. I took what remained and drenched my arm in it. Taking swallows of it to ease the pain as well. I could taste the fire in the back of my throat. A flavor I had been craving since the last time I felt it.

My new friend looked like he wanted some too. I drenched the blade in the bottle of alcohol. The cool liquid made him speak as the bubbles boiled on the still hot blade. It was the same sound he made when he was helping me with my markings. I pulled him out of the liquid after he was done speaking and inspected him closely.

"What is your name?" I asked my new sharp friend.

He was good at fixing my markings and the sounds he spoke reminded of the times I spent with William as he banged his hammer against hot metal and drenched it black water. William was a suitable enough name until he was ready to tell me his own.

"Don't wish to tell me yet?"

He wasn't speaking. He would soon, though.

"Then I will name you after someone you remind me of. I will call you William." I said to him. I stared at him, still inspecting his body. I felt he was curious about the marking he had just carved into me.

"You want to know about my messages? About the markings? Okay…Hmm, where to start?"

It was gray, like everything else appeared to me, but I'd
hear others call it the gray as well, so my sight wasn't
deceiving me. Even William named it The Graylands. It
looked much like this land, but lighter. I could tell when
the sun was alive when I was there. At first I could only
see the land as I peered through the small, circular holes
of William's home. It was the first place I remember
exploring. His home was massive, mostly made from cold
metal and small, dark corridors, often bleeding similar
smoke as my arm.

William was the one who gave me my first marking. He was the first to make me feel a small taste of freedom. He's the one who put metal to blood, and printed the message on my flesh. I still remember it as if it was happening right now, and for all I was concerned, it was the day I was truly born.

I was young then. Weak, small, unskilled. Unaware of what I was or what I was capable of. William had started to let me go out into The Graylands alone. I was exploring the depths of the dead ships that scattered the region. I would follow William when he would travel to them to dismantle pieces of them for his own home.

That's where I met my very first childhood friend. It was a Dweller. Smallest of the Hidden, but William warned me they were still dangerous. Even though it stood on four legs, I could tell the beast was the same size as me—perhaps larger, but not by much. Its long snout, filled with knife-sharp teeth, drooled out a foul liquid.

From its paws emerged organic blades. Its transparent skin covered the organs that moved around inside it. Its many long, tendril-like tails raised at the sight of me as did its thin, hair-like spikes on its body.

Did it want to eat me, or was it defending itself? It didn't matter to me.

At first I toyed with the creature. Playing with it; dancing with it. It was something I had not experienced before—as if my insides are lifting themselves from within me. I'm not sure what it is to this day, but I experience it whenever I am near death. I eventually became bored of the Dweller and it seemed that it was of me as well, as it started to try less and less to kill me. It would snap at me with its sharp, intersecting teeth as I tried to provoke it, but other than that, it would ignore me and run from me. The feeling I felt was gone.

I decided it needed to die.

There were plenty of rusted pieces of metal

that I could kill it with. There were large pipes broken everywhere, but one was broken off to a point. A perfect weapon. I grabbed it and taunted my Dweller friend with it. Finally it pounced once more. I swung the pipe as hard as I could. I hit the Dweller in the head as it leaped at me. I could see its black blood pouring from its face.

The blood excited me. It wasn't red, like I have seen when others bleed, but I wanted to see more of it all the same. I wanted to see more of that rich, blackness that consumed everything around it. My friend was struggling to get back to its feet. I didn't want it to. I took the sharp end of the pipe, and jammed it into its chest. It screamed and spasmed before dying. I knelt down beside my friend as I stared into the thick, oozing fluids as it slowly made all it touched nonexistent. I was so entranced by it that I was not aware that my friend was still moving. It swiped at me with its claws, cutting my abdomen clean open.

I passed out.

It seemed we were both going to die there that day.

I awoke in blinding pain. Unable to breathe, unable to move. William was standing above me jabbing needles into my chest. I gasped for air, but it was a futile attempt.

"Easy now, kid," William said as he continued, repeatedly sliding a needle in and out. "You're gonna make it. Just lie still." He continued wiping my blood from the tiny oozing wounds. "I know it hurts, but this will make you whole again."

I couldn't say anything. I had to just try, in vain, to breathe.

"You're lucky that Dweller didn't finish bleeding out." He said as I continued to choke on my own throat.

"Its blood is going to save your life."

All I could do was stare at him as I gagged, trying

to breathe. I needed to vomit, but I couldn't.

"The blood acts as a neurotoxin. You'll be paralyzed for a while, but I need you to stay awake and try to keep breathing."

I tried as he asked, but breathing wasn't an option. I felt something in my throat, my lungs, and in my mouth. William took his metallic hand and pushed down on my chest with enough force to push out what was caught inside me. My own blood shot from my mouth, covering my face. It was the first time I had seen my own blood. Black, like my friend's. So black that it blinded me. Breathing was easier, but the pain from my open stomach was not.

I was passing out, but William wouldn't allow it.

"I said stay awake." He said in a calm voice as he repeated slapped me.

"All right, Kid. Let me tell you a story…"

His stories. I found myself always listening to his

stories.

"Once upon a time, about thirty years back, there was a mother and her son. They were refugees following the trail down the Northern Pass not far from here. There was a young man with them in a group of a couple of dozen. They were running. Running was all we could do." He stopped to take a swig from a bottle of alcohol. "Running from what people would do to them for what they were."

What *we* were, what *we* are. He said that a lot.

"Night fell before they could find shelter." He continued. "They kept the Hidden at bay with fire, but the boy wandered too far from the light. The young man was able to save the boy, but not before a Hidden bit the young man's arm clean off. Before he had time to react, the mother came to him, and burned a spell into the young man with hot metal. His arm was still gone, but the bleeding stopped. The woman had saved the young man's life, and showed him a way to use his own body to unleash powers only they had."

I started to calm.

"We have always been hunted by those who fear us. We have powers. Powers from the darkness. From the shadows. We are the Wiccan—deemed 'Witches' by others—we have the power to tap into magics using this ancient language."

'We.' I remember him saying that word a lot, too.

"Only Wiccan can tap into it. It's why many hate and fear us." He went on to say, "It's why we hide. It's why we're here."

I could feel my wounds closing. The pain was going away. Soon, it was all gone. I was still paralyzed, but my wounds were gone.

"And it's why right now you're still alive."

He put one of those thick, but small, rolled-up papers in his mouth and lit it as I stared up at him. I could

34

feel the power on my skin. The power to allow my body to repair itself. I listened to William's story. I understood his words.

"Welcome to the club, kid." He said as he clamped onto the rolled paper with his fingers, and let out of breath of smoke. "Population, you and me."

I was finally able to talk, and there only one thing I could say. I slowly turned my head towards him and opened my mouth to speak. It was all I could do.

"More."

Over time William added more and more messages to my body. With each marking that was added, the stronger I became. I became addicted to it. I craved the sensation. But in order to become strong, I had to earn it.

My first marking was the result of killing a Hidden. I had murdered my dark friend, and its blood was used to imprint it on me. It became a ritual. One I found amusing.

For each mark, I have killed a different species of Hidden.

I have journeyed to many lands in search of different kinds, and I will continue to find them until I am satisfied, or there are no more to kill.

William imprinted many different spells onto me. All as useful as the next, but none that weren't without their limits. I remembered each one. I remember when William marked me and what my prey was that earned me the right to have them.

Dwellers.

Of all the Hidden I have killed, Dwellers are by far the most loathsome and despised by man. They also seem to be the most common, and least feared. They are weak by Hidden standards, and only stand as tall as a child when sitting on their back legs.

The Dwellers, like all Hidden, Dwellers bear a black, translucent skin with many spike-like fibers that grow all over its body. They have sharp claws on its four legs that it uses to kill its prey. They have long snouts that protrude past its skin, and large, deadly teeth. At the other end of the beast is a long, thin tail that divides into three smaller tails at the end.

After killing a Dweller, William marked me with the power to heal my wounds. Within moments, a fatal laceration or broken bone will be restored like new. It requires my own blood to work, however, and leaves me weak for some time after being used.

Lurkers.

They are my favorite of the Hidden I have met so far. Flying high above in the clouds. Skin and fur so black they fade into the dark skies. It's nearly impossible to find a Lurker on its own as they hunt in groups by the hundreds.

Knowing exactly what a lurker looks like is difficult as they mostly stay in the skies and any being that is close enough to see is usually already dead. I remember seeing my first one. I got a quick glimpse of it before the rest of them set upon it. Dark and big. Much larger than a human. They have long, flat protruding snouts, large enough to fit most of a fully grown human inside. Their wings are so thin, you can almost see the other side of them, and an equally thin wing on the edge of their tails.

After killing a Lurker William gave me the mark with the power to summon the winds, which I can use to slow my descent and prevent harm from falls, allowing me to explore. However, it takes time to for the winds to come, so the spell will not shield me from injury from lower heights.

Ravines.

The Ravine was a fun fight. Large beasts that stand on both two and four legs. It has a somewhat similar shape as that of a common dog. Jutting snouts, pointed ears, long tails, and similar hind legs. But that is where the similarities end. Its 'hairs' are more like large thorns, its razor teeth overlap their snouts, which are only used as weapons as it eats its food whole. The strangest of all is the Ravine's ability to change its size and shape at will. It is massive in its normal shape, but will expand its body if threatened by a larger creature, or to swallow its prey. Despite their size, they are still extremely fast, and overpowers its victims through sheer force and brutality.

Shooting the Ravine is tough, but their flesh is as susceptible to projectiles as any other kind of flesh. With its blood, William gave me the power to summon fire at will. A useful ability for someone who travels these blackened lands.

Terrauns are interesting creatures. The only Hidden I have found to be stationary. They appear to enjoy swamp lands, seemingly growing into the land as if the Earth, itself, was manifesting them. Pulsating, vein-like limbs pierce from beneath, and climb up whatever it can get its veins on. No one knows if there is more to the creature, but they are extremely deadly. If one is unlucky enough to be stabbed with one of its many spikes, your body will become an organic time bomb. You will swell until you burst, and what remains of you will be absorbed by the Terraun.

Terrauns are hard to kill, but I find fire works best on them. Lots and lots of fire. For killing one, William marked me with the power to go unseen by my foes by tapping into their memory. However, this one has quite a few drawbacks.

It only works on intelligent creatures, such as humans and Giants. And since the markings are on my hands, I can only use the spell on two things at a time. This power also causes me to see the history of the one I'm using it on whether I want to or not.

Ah, the Quagmires. Much like the Terrauns, Quagmires love the swamps as well, but they are much more active when it comes to hunting prey, lurking deep within the murky waters. I should know. I was inside one for a while.

Giant beasts with long tentacles that it uses to

trap and squeeze their prey to death. Each tentacle grows large pustules filled with an acidic substance that can easily burn through flesh. In the center of the tentacles is the main body of the creature. A grotesque blob of black spikes and an enormous mouth with a tunnel of spiked teeth capable of swallowing several men whole.

Of all of the Hidden I have faced, the Quagmire was the closest to killing me. The hunt was tough, but I am still here, and it is not. William used the Quagmire's blood to give me a power with a very unique effect.

The Hidden are practically blind. The only thing they can see is light and all creatures, except the Hidden, emit light. The stronger a light is, the more a Hidden is afraid of it. Most creatures do not give off enough light to keep the Hidden away, but William's marking makes my light stronger. It allows me to travel among The Hidden. They are frightened of me.

This power also grants me another ability: to see

as The Hidden see. To see my enemy's light from great distances and even see them through walls. It's because of this that The Hidden are so good at hunting their prey. It's why this city is devoid of human life.

William helped me kill the Hidden. He showed me how to collect the blood and how to repair the markings when I needed. He taught me how to fire weapons and how to defend myself. He taught me how to kill with whatever I could get my hands on; how to climb and navigate the lands. He taught me to how to fuse metal and how to wield my messages. Most of all, he taught me how to hide. How to blend in and act 'normal'.

He taught me when it was okay to kill.

Most things I caught on to easily and learned

the crafts fairly quickly. Weapons and fighting seemed to be the easiest for me. Whenever I learned something, William seemed to like it, as he'd smile at me. I remember first learning what that was.

I recall the two of us on the bow of his home. He was teaching me how to fire his revolver by firing at a flock of birds near the edge of the plateau. After many tries I was finally able to hit one. William congratulated me and his mouth stretched oddly across his face to the point his teeth were showing.

"Did I do something wrong?" I asked. His smile slowly fading.

"Course not," he replied. "Couldn't have done better, myself."

"Why do you want to attack me?" I asked him. He let out a quick huff of air.

"I hadn't planned on it," he said as his face went back to normal. "Why?"

"Your teeth," I said to him. "Creatures show them to me before they attack."

William grunted and smiled again. "No kid, that's a smile," he replied in a louder voice. "When people do it, it's a good thing."

It was the first time he had started to teach me how to hide in plain sight. How to pretend to be as habitual as others. A skill I am not fond of learning.

I find myself recalling memories involving William and my younger self quite often. I recall reliving them in my mind as I rested my body, and just before I rested my mind. I even found myself returning to his home high up in the Plateaus as if I was supposed to. I did not understand why, but I did not care. Understanding was not needed. I still did it, no matter what.

No matter how long it's been since I last saw the old man, I can still remember every detail about him. William was always illuminated in the heated metal of

47

his blackened, steel rooms. He would forge the metal, mending it as he saw fit. Bending it to his will with his heavy hammer and his machine that always burned with a fierce light. The smell of embers and melted steel covered his home in a heavy, charred mist. All resonating from the metal that we found together. I mostly just watched, but often he would ask for my hand. There were times even the hands he made with his messages could not replace real ones.

I have seen other old people on my path, but none as capable as William. When I was a child, he would stand nearly three of me high when he stood upright. Legs and arms like tree limbs. As I see him now, he only stands maybe less than two of me. The last time I saw him, he was still very thin. I remember even when I was little that my wrists would touch if I wrapped my arms around his waist.

William was not whole. He was missing a few

of his limbs. He only had one full arm. From the elbow down his left arm was missing. His right eye was also gone, made true by my own teeth. Even though he had both of his legs, he still walked with a limp. His long, gray hair reached to his shoulders, and met the length of his equally long beard. At first, I assumed all Wiccan had gray hair, until he told me his wasn't always gray. I wondered if mine wasn't always gray too. I couldn't remember.

His apparel often changed, but he always seemed to be wearing some kind of leather. Even when I couldn't see him, I could still smell the odor of hide in the air that let me know he was around. When forging steel, he would wear a metal mask, or a pair of rounded glasses that completely shielded his eyes. When not within the smoke, he often left his torso bare revealing his toned muscles.

What fascinated me most were the markings on his skin that danced and played across his body like insects moving across the ground, only stopping to form

49

into messages whenever he needed them. I watched as he would mold a metal hand out of scrap and tools to replace his missing one. I watched him lift objects with ease that were impossible for me to budge. I watched him fall from his home, only to soar back up like a winged creature. I have watched as fire consumed him, yet emerged with his flesh still intact.

William's body seemed to constantly be covered in varying conditions of the Gods. It was hard for me to remember a time the smoke didn't consume him in some way. His magic engulfed him whenever he used it. His machines clouded my sight of him with their own magics.

And then there were the things he called his 'one true pleasure.' Pieces of thick, dark paper that trapped two Gods together. Fire and Earth. He breathed the two in, as his mouth would stretch across his face. I think he called them cigars.

My memories of William faded as the sounds

of the Gods rumbling the skies took over my senses. Their sounds were loud and familiar. The dust picked up and became a part of the sky. The sky was black and the Gods were far away. I could not see them but I could hear them. I could feel them. The earth quaked beneath me. Vibrating, shaking as if from fear of them. There was little I could do if they decided to enter the city.

I was completely paralyzed, but despite being outside, I was still safe from the Gods for now. Though the Lurkers from high above were not. As the winds blew with tremendous force, the ground rattled with aching terror and the sky circled the land, the Lurkers found themselves in the Gods' wrath. They panicked, like any mindless animal would.

I watched as the sky suddenly, and quickly came alive as the Lurkers scattered in fear, and the Gods claimed their rightful place. I found myself watching the two battle with great ferocity. It was something there is no word for… I wonder how many will die trying to escape. It wouldn't be right to take from one that the Gods have killed. I needed to kill my own, but for now my markings were sated.

The dust was now a part of the emptiness. It made everything hard to see. The Lurkers that survived were gone. The rest lay dead, scattered across the land. The Gods had settled once again. The dust that covered the ground was now a part of the wind. The darkness was no longer moving. All was quiet—but I remained. Do the Gods favor me? Doubt it. I just know how to avoid them.

As my body began to come back into my control, I took refuge in what would be my new shelter for what time I was there. I sat at the empty second story window of the canteen drinking from my container of water, wondering if the Lurkers would come back. There was something off about not seeing them. The quiet also set me into a cautious state. While I could find solace in the silence, creatures are always the quietest when a predator is nearby.

I was certain I was alone here. I had scoured nearly a half mile of the city with nothing but remnants of life, yet I couldn't shake off that someone or something was around me. I looked around, both in and out of the building, scanning what little I could see of the land for anything. It didn't take long to find it, but once I saw it, I could not take my eyes away from it.

I could see it as clear as day. A light within the thickness of the air. Despite all of the dust, dirt, and debris in the air, there it was as clear as day. A strange thing to see in a city populated by the dead and myself. It seemed a tiny bit of the city was still alive. The veins were still flowing, even now. Dim and faint, but flowing, nonetheless.

Did someone turn this light on? Am I not the only being here? Perhaps survivors, or maybe scavengers, like me. Either way, they were potential threats. All those who remain in this land survive by being predators.

I had pondered whether or not to find them before they found m—

...but then I saw it.

7

What I saw was the absence of light. A shadow casting
in front of the light that I found myself staring at.
Pondering at. It was moving. Slowly, but moving,
nonetheless… It was alive. As it moved about, I could see
less of the light, nearly covering the it entirely as it passed.
It was a window, and as far as it was, I could still make out
parts the shadow. A head on top of a massive, slouching
body.

The more I looked at it, the more clear I could
see it. It must have been a giant. Had to be. I could now

see its bulbous arm swaying and its gigantic shoulders that connected to its relative small sized head. What kind of giant, I couldn't tell, but there was no way this shadow could possibly be cast by anything else.

I stared at the light, as well as at the giant for a while. The giant had been moving from one side to the other, as if searching for something. Minutes would pass before I saw it again.

Then seconds…

Then minutes again…

I wondered what this giant—this shadow—was doing, but then it stopped in front of the light. I could see it standing there, facing the window. It was now motionless, lifeless. I think this giant found what it was searching for.

I realized I had mistakenly left the lights on behind me. This thing was looking at me. No, not at me. It was looking at my darkness, as I was his. I stared at it for as long as it chose to stare back at me. What was it doing? Was it sizing me up? Looking to see if I would back down first? It was as if two predators had entered the same hunting ground and I was not backing down.

As I stared at this thing, I realized it wasn't an ordinary giant. One side wasn't proportional with the other. One side looked much smaller. Almost human. A much smaller arm hung from the rest of this shadow. The rest I was unable to make out, as it formed into one dark blob. I knew this thing wasn't what I thought it was.

Was it human? Was it giant? Was it a Hidden I had yet to discover? Or was it an abomination created by the land itself? These questions had no meaning if they had no answers. What did have meaning, however, were the questions I did have answers to. It wanted to hunt me, and I want to hunt it. It was only a matter of time. Just need the dust to die down.

My eyes began to sting from the dust but I

refused to take my gaze off of this thing for even a second. I refused to break my sight from his darkness. I wanted one brief glance of movement, one brief moment of weakness. It thinks itself a predator, but I'll show it that it is wrong.

Hours passed as I sat crouched in the window, remaining unmoved, unblinking as I stared this creature down. I could tell it was doing the same as I was. Waiting for the dust to clear so our game could begin.

It was time.

The winds vanished, and the dust was settling back down. I leaped from my perch and made my way down the side of the building. I hurried through the streets and allowed my instincts to tell me where to go. I needed to get out of the dust so I began scaling my way up the buildings, becoming a part of the shadows as I leaped from story, to story, using the ridges of the stone created from decay, and the metal that protruded from the broken chunks of the buildings.

I wanted to get as high as I could, but too high would lessen my senses. I kept to about the fifth and sixth stories of the buildings, using my message to call the winds when I needed to leap between them.

As I made it to a high enough elevation, I crouched over to the edge of a window, and watched the light from before.

The darkness was gone. He was on the hunt just as I was. My instincts told me that this thing thinks I am on the run from it. It does not know that this is a game of equal stalkers.

I remained on the edge of the buildings near the light for some time, keeping an eye out for my prey. Watching to see if there was any movement. There wasn't any. No movement but for the dust below. No sound but for the cry of the winds. No smell but for the scent of ash. Either it stayed in the shadows better than I thought a creature of that size would, or it's moving through the structures.

The closer I got to the light, the fewer towering structures there were. I had to make my way down closer to the ground. I leaped from the perch, speeding downwards, my face leading the way. The smoke rose through the wraps around my arm. The smell of copper and sulfur caressed my nostrils. As the wind slowed my fall, I rolled onto the street below.

I was on the ground, but I could still use my markings to detect life though the walls. There was none. I crept through the shadows as I scanned the area. I could see nothing but the stone and brick I had been used to. At first glance, it looked similar to all of the other regions of the city I had seen already—rubble, signs of decay, the markings of former survivors. But this area was different. The structures appeared in greater damage here. Chains and hooks were attached to and hung from seemingly everything. Chains were even stretched across from building to building. The thick odor of blood and decay sang through my senses.

This was very different from the rest of the city.

I followed the scent until it was overwhelming; thinking it would lead to the one I was hunting. It did not lead me to my playmate, but to something even better. Something I had never seen until then. The corpses of what looked to mostly be human were scattered across the area. Hung on gates, fences, pikes, and the various hooks that were attached to the buildings and pillars. Anywhere a body could be skewered, a body was certain to be there. Most of the limbs and heads looked to have been cut or torn from all of them. Only the torsos remained. Both male and female were hung like ornaments. I felt that this was where it liked to play. I felt as if I was peering into the den of my prey. I needed a closer look.

They were everywhere. Too many to count.

Some were fresh, others were rotted to the bone. There was very little blood to speak of, but the streets were littered with the fallen organs. From the condition of the bodies it was clear the Gods have enjoyed them for some time. He must have been at this for decades. Finding scavengers, survivors, and travelers and taking them apart for years.

The scent of human remains consumed the land as much as the sight them engulfed my eyes. It was quiet here. Even the wind was cautious. I looked around wondering if I could count them all. Hundreds? Maybe even close to a thousand. It was hard to tell, as they seemed to go on forever. I had recalled one marking on the wall. It made no sense until now, but now its message was clear.

I had just walked into the city of torsos. It was beautiful. A city filled with torsos. Every last one neatly hung with a sense of joy and pride in them.

These were its trophies, its markings—delicately placed for even the Gods to see, like decorations. I wear mine on my flesh; this thing shows them off for this land to bear witness. How I wish I could envy it. I found myself staring at them, caressing them in wonder.

I had never seen so many dead all at once. They were all unique, each placed in a different fashion, in a different state of decay. I think it wanted me to see them. Why would he not? I'm sure everyone here got to see this before they became part of it. I wondered if they enjoyed seeing this before they died. I was not certain what fascinated me about these corpses but I found myself compelled to touch them.

They were like me—empty, soulless, grayed, and hardened from the ash storms. Some of the flesh crusted and whisked away at my touch. I wondered what it felt about the Gods doing this to them—his messages. Perhaps that's the reason they were here. He liked them this way.

It was like the magic that courses through me. My markings are proof that I am still alive—that I feel alive.

These bodies are proof that he lives too. I was starting to feel a bond with this creature I hunted. Like me, this thing attests his existence through death.

Oh, so much death.

Hours had passed as I explored the bodies. Suddenly
a sharp, painful screech echoed through the roadways.
The pitch was high enough to rattle my teeth. I know
the sound. A familiar sound I have heard many, many
times before. It was metal. Something heavy and metallic
scraping concrete in a slow and long pattern. The sound
took my attention away from the decorations. The sound
was getting more and more faint. It was moving. Was this
sound from the one who placed these bodies here? Was it
the one I was playing with? Had to be.

I followed the sound, making my way back up the derelict structures. The sound was moving away but slowly.

Very slowly.

I knew this giant had its back to me. I could easily scale one of the structures and get a vantage point to see my new friend before he saw me. If I had the upper ground, this hunt would be over before it began.

I was getting closer and closer to the repetitious sound. The closer I got, the more the noise could be better described. The loud screaming of the metal dragging across the surface of the ground vibrated through what was left of me. It was unpleasant to my senses. Even more so to the structures around as they seemingly shook in fear.

I knew I was close. An unfamiliar scent collected in the air. Like a mix between sulfur and rot. I crept to a section of a building that had already partially collapsed. I stayed crouched as I looked out, trying to find the source of the noise. Part of me hoped the source of the noise was not my play mate. How easy it was to find him, and creep up on him. If it was him, there was no fun in this. It was far too unchallenging.

But alas. There he was...

There *it* was.

Flesh consumed with ore-like swellings all over its body. It was *Ahseeni Keywok*. A Rock Giant. Stone Walkers. Humans, and the like had many names for them. Creatures created of both flesh and stone. Skin of gray ash. Large, powerful humanoids with muscles of harden rock-like deformities that protrude from their very skin. But this... this *thing...* could not possibly be a Stone Walker. At least not anymore. It was different. Changed. Deformed.

Calling this creature Ahseeni Keywok seemed wrong. It was more stone than flesh, if you could call it flesh at all. I have heard some call them the beautiful giants, as they appear the most human than any other kind of giant. This thing looked nothing like a human. Not even in shape. Nothing but disdain rose from me as I watched this creature slowly trampling everything in its path. Its long, skinny legs barely able to support its grotesquely misshapen upper half.

It was hunched over, with a malformed, bulging chest, and thin abdomen, which was partially covered by a bloodstained cloak that looked as if it was once a lighter color. It looked masculine, but who could say what it once was. Its boil-like rock protrusions infested its head—that seemed to be petrified into a scream. I couldn't tell if it was its muscles hiding its neck, or the fact that its neck had simply sunken into its chest, but the creature had no visible neck to speak of.

Its most notable deformity was its one tiny, human-sized arm on its left side, and a giant petrified arm—molded in lumps of rock, ash, and blood—on the right that it used to drag along what I could only guess was its weapon.

The weapon was a large, rusted hunk of metal, likely pulled from one of the many abandoned mounts around the city. It looked to stand almost as large as the giant itself, standing over twice as large as me. It had been hammered flat into a solid, thick blade. If you could call it that. To call it a blade didn't seem right. It wasn't sharp. You could just as easily cut with a rounded pipe.

A long chain, similar to the ones used to hang the bodies, was connected to the 'blade.' The chain was rusted and long, wrapping around this creature's body several times. The weapon was huge and seemingly extremely heavy given its strain trying to carry it. I wondered how such a large piece of steel could be used as a reliable weapon.

Upon closer inspection of the metal it carried, I could see faint red mixed into the rust. Dried blood covered the weapon. It must have been the tool it used to hack the limbs from its ornaments. It must have been a long time since its last kill, as the color was faint at best. It must have been happy to have seen me. I must be the first person its seen in quite some time.

I decided to follow it for a time. Keeping myself high above as the creature slowly ambled about the streets, likely trying to make its way to the canteen it saw me in. The thing was often hard to see it, as its flesh was as stone-like as the buildings around it. I started to understand why it made this place its home. Perhaps this is where it felt most comfortable. A city like this was the perfect place for this creature to hide.

And to hunt.

I continued to follow it for a while; it was seemingly unaware that I was stalking it from above. It didn't seem to be going in the direction I came from anymore. In fact, it appeared to just be moving about the streets in random directions, as if its mind was completely gone. Had it forgotten about me? Was this really the playmate I was looking for? Was this the creature that had made all of those ornaments? I almost felt disappointed.

I was certain it saw me, that it wanted me, but there was no thrill, no excitement in hunting this beast. It didn't even seem to be hunting me at all anymore. Just floating about the dust like a noisy ghost. Had I waited too long? Perhaps this creature's mind was also distorted to the point of an animal.

'Such a waste,' I thought to myself as I sighed.

I should just put this monster down. Put it out of its misery, and move on. I have all I came here for. I should leave while the Gods are quiet, and it'd only be a matter of time before they returned.

I watched the creature hobble about the cracked concrete as I decided how to end it. Azathoth might not have the power to punch through all that stone flesh.

Close range combat was not an option either. While not impossible to kill a giant up close, this thing was more armored than a normal one. Getting close to this thing would surely result in my death.

"Sothoth… it's your time to let the blood flow," I said as pulled Sothoth from his sheath. "Make me proud."

I took aim, ready to let Sothoth's hand soar. The giant let out a loud moan—a sound much like that of a crying child. Was it pity I should be feeling right now? I forget a lot of the words William taught me. No matter. This creature shouldn't exist. It was impure, an abomination that needed to be destroyed. Created from magics or science that had no right to be.

Many saw the same in me.

I pulled his trigger. Sothoth sang his familiar song. The loud, crisp explosion that I've grown to enjoy. And just as Azathoth did, Sothoth sang true. His bullet burrowed deep into the creature's armored flesh. It was only a matter of time before his little hand sang its own song while deep inside the creature. Ending its life for good.

Any time now...

Sothoth? ...So-o-o-o-o...thoth... Time to wake up...

His hand stayed mute. No song was sung. The shot was a dud. The creature was still alive and very much aware of my presence now. It looked at me, much like it did when it was just a shadow. I wasn't sure what it was going to do.

The creature surprised me with its speed. Before my mind could process it, the creature had slung its large weapon at me. The blade embedded itself into the wall below me. I looked at the creature, and gave him a smile in acceptance. Perhaps I would get the fight I was looking for after all.

Using its larger arm, the creature pulled on the

chain that was connected to the handle of the weapon. The force caused the floor I was standing on to topple over. I fell from my vantage point and plummeted to the ground.

I summoned the wind, and the smell of smoke rose from my arm. The smoke lifted into the air as I floated down. I landed in the middle of the road on my feet, with one hand on the stone, and the other carrying Sothoth. I reached for Azathoth and readied the both of them.

I couldn't see the creature at first. The rubble causing dust to pick up, clouding my vision. I could no longer hear the metal dragging against the ground. Instead I could smell the creature now. It was more than enough to track it. My friends and I were ready for whatever it may have in mind for us.

The dust was beginning to clear. It came around the corner of one of the buildings, carrying its weapon across its shoulder. It stopped in the middle of the road on the other end of the building. The dust had only cleared enough for me to see its shadow again.

Could it see me? Maybe it could see my shadow as I could see its. I was crouched, low to the ground, so maybe it was looking for me. With Azathoth and Sothoth in my hands, I was ready for whatever this thing had. The dust finally cleared, and I could finally see it. I could see its eyes for the first time.

I smiled. William always told me to smile whenever you looked at someone in the eyes.

"Hey," I said to it. It didn't return the pleasantry.

Perhaps it needed William to teach it, too.

The creature's speed amazed me yet again. I could only make Azathoth sing a couple times before it was on me. I rolled out of the way just as its weapon descended. The weapon cracked the earth, throwing it into the air. The strength and power behind this thing's swings was not surprising. I knew it could obliterate me in just one direct hit. But I could use its strength to my advantage.

After pulling its weapon from the broken asphalt, it began swinging wildly. Over and over the creature swung at me, in hope one would strike me. No such luck, my friend, as you are not the only fast one here. I dodged the first few swings, but eventually I had to back away. I watched as the it violently swung over and over, seemingly unaware I was no longer near.

The giant was in a blind rage. No longer fixed on me, but focused on destroying everything nearby. Gates, walls, the ground below its feet. It didn't seem to matter what it hit. As he swung his massive weapon, debris began to flood the streets. I took the time while it raged to enter one of the nearby buildings and made my way up the mostly stable stairs.

The second floor had many pillars and walls still intact, but there was still enough space to move about.

"Hm," I pondered.

For a giant, this place would be narrow, confined. But for a small being like me? Yes, I could fight just fine here. It was the perfect place to trap him. These pillars would limit the use of its weapon. Giving me the chance to take this beast by surprise.

It followed me into the building. I crept along the second floor, watching from above from the missing sections of the floor. I wondered how it was tracking me. I was only one level above it. It was so close I could reach out and touch the top of its head, but it didn't seem to smell me. I wanted to test it. See how long it took to find me if I hid in plain sight.

I crept back to the stairs as silently as possible and took a seat on the middle step. I watched it scramble about the first floor, unable to find me.

How well could it see? I wondered. *Its sight must be be limited. Maybe only able to see movement and light. If I do not move, if I remain the the dark, it cannot see me.*

I inspected its swollen face further. One of its eyes was mostly covered in rock. The other didn't appear to have an eyelid. Just a big, round, bloodshot gray... *thing*. Clearly it didn't hunt by sight.

Could it climb?

Surely a monster this large and asymmetric couldn't possibly climb, but with its ability to throw its weapon with so much force, climbing might not be the smartest tactic.

The only other conclusion I could make was that it was tracking me by sound. I could use this to confuse it, but I needed to make sure.

I whistled. The creature turned its head in my direction.

That was it. He heard me.

It bolted towards me like a wild animal. He was far enough away that I was long gone before he crashed into the concrete wall. It destroyed a portion of the stairs as well, so I took my time. I rested my back on one of the pillars as I waited for my massive friend to ascend the broken steps.

As I waited, I ruminated on what the best tactic was to kill this creature. Azathoth and Sothoth were loyal, but they sang loudly. William the knife may not be strong enough to pierce its hardened flesh. My best option was to get it trapped in here and hope Sothoth feels like singing a full song this time.

I watched as it lumbered up the steps and slowly searched the floor for me.

I watched as it passed right by me.

I waited for it to pass before I took Azathoth and used the bottom of her handle to tap on the pillar behind me.

Almost instantly, the creature slammed its weapon into the pillar, making a thunderous crash. Dust and debris poured over me. I could feel the hunk of metal just behind my head. It was time to make my move. It's time to redeem yourself, Sothoth.

I moved from behind the pillar and fired Sothoth several times into the creature. The creature flailing its weapon, only able to strike the pillars around it. Sothoth was damaging my friend, but the power of his explosive shells were not doing enough damage to kill it out right.

I hid behind a pillar as it came for me. Its stone flesh now cracked by Sothoth. Embers still radiating from the cracks. I needed to reload my old friends, but my new one would surely hear me. I wondered if I could plunge William into one of the cracks in its chest. If I hit the heart, I could kill it.

I quietly slid Azathoth back into her sheath, and slowly removed William from his. As the creature was slamming its weapon into the pillars or one of the few walls, I waited for it to get stuck again. When it did, I quickly darted toward the creature, leaped into the air, and drove William's blade as deeply as I could into its heart.

I looked into its eye. I knew it could see me now, though unchanging. I wanted to look this thing in the eyes as it died. I wanted so much for it to feel fear as it looked back into mine. I wanted it to know its life was in my hands. To know that it was the prey. Not me. But I saw none of that.

I saw no fear, no pain.

Just emptiness.

This abomination didn't hate me. It didn't appear to feel anything at all. It only attacked me, hunted me out of instinct. I only realized that after looking this creature directly into its eyes that I was reminded of the mirror I looked into before in the canteen. This mutilated thing was like me. A kindred spirit. It was then all of my interest in this creature arose once more. I was starting to feel alive again playing with my friend.

William was lodged deep in its chest. Only the hilt was still visible. As hard as I tried, I was unable to remove him. The creature wasted no time grabbing me, and slinging me into a wall, but not before slamming me into an already damaged pillar, completely shattering it. I hit the floor like a rag doll, and slid across the dust-covered cement. The creature was already coming for me before I could make sense of what happened.

The creature was fast, but clumsy. It crashed through many of the pillars. Its metal striking them down one by one as it came for me. That's when I noticed the dust falling from above me. I looked up and saw the cracks forming in the ceiling. They were increasing in size the more the creature tore down the pillars holding it up.

I leaped to the side as the creature swung at me. I hid behind another pillar and waited for it to get quiet and the dust to clear. Once all was silent, It began looking around for me again. I took Sothoth and slammed the bottom of his handle on the nearby wall. The beast lunged toward me. I could hear him coming at me from behind the wall, but the first thing I saw was it massive blade piercing the wall only inches from me. I rolled away and outran the blade as it made quick work of the wall.

Again, I struck another wall, and again, it smashed through it with enough force to split it in half. The sound of falling rubble began to confuse the creature. It began to randomly swing its weapon in every direction. I began banging on the pillars and walls to guide it where I wanted.

I continued to force it to destroy every pillar until there were none left. The ceiling above began to rumble, and dissect. Large chunks began to collapse. The creature continued to attack at random. The sound of falling rock confused its senses. The ceiling was about to fall and take us both with it. It was time to leave.

I leaped from one of the empty windows just as

the building seemed to swallow itself. The rubble was crushing the enraged creature. I hit the ground rolling. I stayed kneeling as I watch a large section of the building collapse in on itself. I watched as the third floor became the second floor. Then the fourth floor became the second, then the fifth. It made a thunderous music that I found myself found of.

Soon, what was left of the building toppled over, hitting the building next to it. The impact caused both structures to start breaking apart. Large pieces of the two structures began to fall to the ground, making the world itself growl beneath my feet and the sky crash with thunder above me. The collapse threw dust in the air so thick it became hard to breathe. My clothes, face, and hair were now covered in a thick layer of it.

Cough.

I watched for movement as the dust persisted. There was nothing. No movement, no sound, no smell but the overwhelming scent of dust and ash. I kept looking for something.

Watching.

Waiting.

I waited for anything to tell me if my friend was alive, but there was nothing. It was silent again. The hunt was unfortunately over, it seemed. I felt empty again. It's almost instant. The feeling never lasts. There was nothing left for me to do here. I hate it when boredom sinks in. It's an uncomfortable sensation. I should leave now. Nothing left but what the Gods decide to keep.

I made my way through the streets, realizing that I no longer had William with me.

It seems I had lost two friends today.

After paying my respects to my fallen friends, I set off once again. I came to a crossroad. This particular area had a large mass of derelict steel mounts. To the right of me, the road ended in a deep, black crevice as if the land itself gave way. To the front was a barrier of mounts stacked on top of each other. It looked more like a pile of metal bars and wheels. None were still intact. While I was tempted to just climb the mass of metal and rubber, I needed to give my body time to recover. The left was the only path without any resistance.

I could hear something. I couldn't tell where it was coming from. The sound seemed to come from everywhere at once. A loud creaking. I stopped and scanned the area. I could see something moving to the right of me. The movement was accompanied by a shrieking moan of metal. I looked to see one of the mounts sliding off into the blackness. Why was it moving now? Had I disturbed its slumber somehow?

I felt a jerking against my leg. I looked down to see my leg was caught on a long rusted chain. As the mount started to fall the chain began to snap forward. At the end of the chain was a small hook that pierced the back of my leg. The chain dragged me across the asphalt before snapping upward, taking me with it.

The mount hit the bottom of the crevice causing a loud crash of metal and glass. I was trapped, hanging high off the ground, upside down. The sound of more crashing and thunder caught my attention. It came from the two collapsed buildings. The playground I had so much fun in before.

I could see it again. A shadow I was very familiar with now. A familiar shape, a familiar size, a familiar sound.

It was coming for me.

Slowly, it was coming for me—its weapon now hitting the ground, making that shrill cry. This hunt wasn't over and now I was the prey caught in its trap. As I saw my friend and gave it a smile.

"Hey."

My friend threw its weapon at me with great force. I could watch it spinning through the air, gracefully cutting through the dust. I watched as it came closer and closer, until I heard the snap. The blade cutting through my leg. I felt it tear through my flesh. I could feel it hitting and severing the bone clean in half. Having my leg severed freed me. I fell to the ground, my back taking the impact. I looked at what remained of my left leg. I wanted to see it.

The black blood and smoke rose from the wound. The blood spurted ever so gently from my veins. The smoke dissipated as it rose and blended with the dust. The pain was so great I thought for a moment I could feel something. As I started to fade away. I saw my friend coming for me. Its footsteps getting louder and louder. As much as I enjoyed the pain, the loss of blood was too much. I was blacking out... But before I did, I almost felt happy for a...

very...

brief...

second...

I recalled a time with William, as I often do when my body gives out, of one of the first times I had experienced a society. I had not thought something so strange existed for a very long time. The idea of people working and living together is a concept I still don't quite understand, but finding items is easier the more people are around, so it is tolerable.

I remembered William not only looking differently, but acting differently whenever we were around other people. His clothes were different. He wore a long leather coat and his markings would glide behind his back, concealing them. He would also wrap mine in cloth. I didn't understand why he did it. He even insisted we wear them when not inside his home.

When we entered the first settlement (as William called them) many of the people kept to themselves. Eyes, down or looking forward, like ghosts walking the roads. I didn't see the point to hiding ourselves if no one bothered to look. But then I noticed something as I stared at the different people. As I stared at them, they would look and stare back. The first one to do that was an old woman who had before been looking down as she walked the side of the road. I had wondered if her insides were red. I wanted to find out. While lost in the idea, she looked up and stared at me with a look I've learned to recognize as disdain.

I didn't understand at first. How did she know I was looking at her? It wasn't until he explained it to me.

"Don't stare, kid." He said as he grabbed me by the arm. "People pick up on that shit."

At the time, I was confused as to what shit he was talking about, but by the smell, I figured there was plenty around.

"Stay close and don't stare."

How did he know I was looking at them? I was walking behind him and he definitely was not looking back at me. "How did you know?"

"Look around," William said as I circled my field of view, seeing even more looking in my direction. "They're all looking. Just stay by me and keep your eyes to yourself."

William put his arm around my shoulder as we continued down the muddy road.

"People know it when you look at them too long," he explained. "Others pick up on it."

"Should I kill them?" I asked.

"What are the rules, kid?" He said looking down at me. I didn't reply at first. "Say them to me. Keep looking forward and repeat them back to me."

I took a moment to remember the rules. There were so many, and they all confused me.

Rule one.

"Only kill to defend yourself."

Rule two.

"Only kill out of necessity."

Rule three.

"Only kill to defend others."

Rule four.

"Only kill if they have killed."

"And?" William asked with a slight pitch to his voice. I thought for a moment, but I couldn't remember the last one. William stopped and looked down at me.

"Rule five. If not defending yourself or another, never... *never* kill in public."

Strange that the only rule that made sense to me was the one I forgot. If one sees me kill, the others might organize to kill me. It's something I've experienced before, and something I would not forget.

"Keep that one in mind while we're here, got me?" William stared until I nodded my head in response.

"Good," he said smiling at me. I couldn't help but notice that he could stare at me, but not at others. I remained silent for the time, trying to remember all of the rules. I ran them through my head, trying to make sense of them.

I kept my eyes down for the rest of the time, as any time someone crossed my field of view the thought of seeing their blood would infect my mind. The urge was too strong, but I didn't want to disappoint William.

We continued on the roads, occasionally turning down another, until we reached a set of buildings with lots of varied shapes and sizes of metal- -sheets, plates, pipes, and other large, heavy-looking metal objects stacked on top of each other nearly as tall as the buildings themselves.

I remember William going straight toward one human—I assumed he was human—he was tall, but tiny by giant standards. His limbs were not deformed, nor was his skin pale or dark, like Yakshi. He had to be human.

Though, I had no idea what he actually was. I couldn't feel him, so he wasn't Wiccan. It didn't matter. I didn't want to hunt him as William seemed fond of him.

"William!" The man said walking towards him. "Fuck! What happened to your eye?"

William smiled, then looked at me. Then he looked back at the man. I understood. I was the one who bit it out. I wasn't sure what else to do so I bared my teeth too. The man was stained in a dark fluid. He smelled strong, pungent like alcohol, which I assumed was coming from the fluid all over his clothes. I had seen William in a similar fluid a few times. His face and clothes were layered with a thick smut and dirt. His face cringed when he saw me 'smile.'

"Just an accident," William replied.

"It's been a while," the man said grabbing and shaking William's hand. William didn't seem to mind.

"Been busy with a project," William said letting go of his hand. The man looked down at me.

"I'll say," he said staring at me. I stared back at first, but then looked away remembering what William told me. "Who'd you knock up?"

William smiled again, and let out his breath. He then grabbed the man by the shoulder and they both started walking away.

"I was hoping you could help me with something," William said to the man. "I need a few components to an engine and about ten lines of two and a half-sized steel pipe."

As they walked away, William stopped and turned to look at me. "Stay right there, kid."

I did as he told while they talked to each other. I was out of earshot, so I didn't know what they were saying. I continued standing there while they walked about the area, looking at the stacks of metal. I watched them, unsure of what else to do. As I watched I couldn't help but notice how much William was staring at this human, and smiling as he did. They also touched a few times, slapping each other's shoulders, and making weird sounds with their mouths as they smiled with their mouths open. That I now know is called laughing. Was William breaking his own rule? I was confused.

Eventually both William and the human touched hands and shook again. William began walking back towards me.

"I'll have it delivered to you by next sundown," the human yelled to William with his hands cupped around his mouth. William simply turned raised his one hand up with his thumb up in the air.

"Ready to go?" William asked once I was in earshot.

I didn't say anything. A look of concern grew as he came closer. He knelt down and touched my shoulder.

"Everything all right, kid?"

I avoided eye contact.

"You can look at someone when they're talking to you."

I looked up at him.

"You were acting strangely around that human," I said to him. "You touched, smiled at him, and stared at him."

William smiled. Then I realized he was doing all the same to me. Touching my shoulder, staring at me, and smiling. "It's because we're friends."

"Are we friends?"

He hesitated for a moment. "Yeah, kid," he replied. "Yeah, we are."

I awoke. Vision blurred from all the blood I lost. The pain from my missing leg had subsided for the most part. The blood had stopped but the gaping wound my leg once was was far from healed. I was lying against flat, cold metal, and unable to move. Too weak. My friend must have assumed I was dead. Otherwise, it would have finished me off or bound me to the metal somehow. It didn't matter if it had or not. My body was heavy. Too heavy to move. I wasn't going anywhere.

I could feel, smell the smoke rising from my chest.

Seems my message was keeping me alive while my mind was gone. My vision was clearing, and I felt my breath return to me. It would be some time before I regained my ability to move, but at least now I could turn my head with relative ease.

As my vision began slowly coming back to me, I saw Azathoth and Sothoth, along with much of my other equipment on a metal table not far from me. They may as well have been miles away, however. Try as I might, all my body was capable of were a few futile twitches and spasms.

I could finally see my surroundings. The room was all black around me, a bright light above me. The light was familiar. As if I had seen it before. I could feel the wind blowing through my hair. I could only see the top, but there was a window directly behind me. This light was the light I saw from before. The first time I had seen my friend's shadow.

The smell of dried blood was overwhelming—
almost too strong for my senses to bear. The room was
large. Big enough for a giant to walk comfortably around.
All about me there were metallic tables circling me with
various tools laying on top and hanging from above.
Nearly everything in the room screamed with the faint
appeal of crimson and rust.

There was but one sound I could hear. The far
off sound of rock and metal grinding together. A familiar
sound, but this time it was different. This time it was
constant... lighter. I could smell my friend nearby along
with the scent of heated metal.

Then I could see it. The shadow of my friend
—a shadow I had grown fond of seeing—on the other
side of this room for giants. It had its weapon in hand,
sharpening it on a large grinder. For a weapon that large,
it must have been grinding for a long time before I awoke.
Long enough for the metal to heat from the friction

alone. It must have been dulled from so much use.

I listened to that sound for what seemed like hours. Time always slowed for me when nothing interesting was happening. But eventually my friend rose from its seat, and turned to face me. Thank the Gods… I was getting so bored.

It slowly lumbered toward me until it finally stood in the light. I could see it. It was right there… looking at me; William the Knife still lodged in its chest. There they stood before me. Two friends I thought I had lost. My large friend stood there staring at me as it walked around me. Slowly moving about, often switching its attention from the tools it had laying about, to me. Even slouching over me, inches from my body, seemingly *inspecting* me. Or perhaps admiring me. I watched as it examined me—its new trophy soon to become a part of his message.

It dawned on me that I didn't know its name, so I

asked.

"What's your name?" It didn't reply, only making heavy breaths as it continued.

"Don't know?" I continued. "Would you like for me to give you one?"

I thought about it for a little while. Thinking back to all of its many decorations that I was so fascinated with, and the words I had read on the walls. 'The Torso's it read'. 'Beware The Torsos,' 'Welcome to the City of Torsos.' It seemed the most fitting name above all.

"I will call you, Torsos," I said to it with a smile.

Torsos said nothing back. Instead, it stopped to the right of me, and reached over with its one giant hand. Torsos didn't even have to lean as it picked up an object from a steel table to the left of me. Trying to see what was in its hand, I realized it had already removed the clothes from my upper body. It'd removed my torn, black poncho and my black shirt of wired mesh. It had removed my glove, and my scarf, leaving only the wraps covering my markings.

As I listened to it breathing more deeply, its smaller left arm began to caress my chest and stomach, especially taking great interest in the area from which smoke lifted through the wraps. Any chance the arm got, it was touching me, often twitching as it did. As I looked on, I could see the arm very clearly. It was thin, delicate, feminine. As if from a woman. The left arm seemingly acted independently from the right.

While one arm seemed to be interested more in touching me, the other was preparing me for the slaughter. I didn't have to reach into Torsos' mind to know what the creature wanted once I saw what was in his right hand. A knife. At least by Torsos' scale, it could be considered a knife. For me, it was more like an over-sized machete, although I wasn't able to see it entirely.

It didn't bother removing my lower clothing. It

didn't need to. It had no interest in my legs. I was to be its newest ornament to be mounted with the rest of them. There was a part of me that felt honored to have that privilege.

"You want me to be a part of your playground, do you?" I asked as it turned its back to me, grabbing other tools and laying them on the table my body was resting on. "I saw them. Your messages. They were magnificent."

Again Torsos said nothing back. I didn't expect it to at this point. All I could do was watch and wait as it placed more and more tools beside me. Did it need all of them to take me apart, or could it not decide which to use?

I could feel my strength starting to come back to me. I could move my hands, but not enough to do anything. If I could stall Torsos for just a moment, my body would be mine again, but so far it didn't seem to notice anything I said. Clearly Torsos' mind was focused on one thing and nothing would interrupt it.

Torsos, with its delicate hand, took my arm by the hand and extended it to the side. Took the end of my wraps, and began to to unwrap them. The feminine hand began to twitch even more as it removed them. All I had left covering my top half were the wraps around my chest.

When it was finished unraveling the thin cloth, I could see them. There they were—my markings, there for Torsos to see. It was only fair. I had seen its field of bodies, so it had every right to look at mine. The creature's eyes were the first to see them other than William and myself.

Torsos was staring at them. Its small hand beginning to twitch and spasm sporadically. Was it the sight of my markings? Did it recognize them? Does it know what I am?

It let out a scream. An ear-piercing scream that shook my body. The scream was indiscernible from human, or Stone Walker. Male or female. It was screeching, deafening, incomprehensible.

Torsos was no longer admiring me. No. Instead, it was cringing at the sight of me. It had gained a fear of me that I had not thought possible for this creature. Was it the markings, or did it have a natural fear of Witches? It didn't matter. Torsos picked up one of the massive blades from the table with me, and it swung it downward onto my arm.

I watched as the hunk of steel severed my arm in one clean cut. I felt the shake of the ground below me as weapon gave way, and Torsos' giant fist rumbled the cold, concrete floor. I stared as more of my blood poured from my body. I could smell it. Like gun powder and sulfur.

I held my breath. The surge of pain going up through my nerves was nothing short of amazing. I looked up as I felt a smile draw across my face. I lay holding my breath, basking in the pain until I couldn't anymore, and I let it out in one single, wheezing breath.

And then suddenly, my body did something it hadn't done before. An involuntary reaction to the pain, I guessed. It came from my chest, like a gust of wind had built up in my lungs and had to be let out. It was light, but I could not stop it from exiting my lips. I've heard others do this before, but I had never experienced it myself. I didn't think my body was capable of it. I think the humans I heard do it call it...

laughing...

I was laughing.

Torsos grabbed my arm from the now-fractured floor. It turned his back to me and lay my arm on a bloody table. I could see it grabbing the large blade that laid beside me. The knife was as rusted and bloody as everything else in the room with one difference over all the other blades—this one had a hook. Something I had seen before. It was a skinning blade.

That was my arm. Those were my markings. Proof of all the Hidden beasts I'd killed. They were a part of me, and all Torsos wanted was to destroy them. I couldn't let it take my messages from me. Not while I was still alive.

While it had my arm, it did not have all of my markings. Some still remained on my chest, but those weren't important. There was one it neglected to see. The marking of the hidden eye in the palm of my hand. Both my hands carried this mark, but I only needed the one. I could use the mark to peer into its mind, and erase his sight of me. I would be invisible to it and to it alone.

I could feel more of my body returning to me. My muscles releasing me from their grasp, setting me free to do as I pleased. I could move my arm again. I could move once more. I could see Torsos beginning to cut the flesh

111

of my arm. Just a few more seconds, and my body would completely be mine again.

The healing was done and the smoke dissipated from my skin. The moment I was able, I quickly sat up, and raised my arm toward it with an open palm. It just needed to look at the eye, and I would be able to see what it sees, know what it knows.

In my haste to get up, I ended up knocking one of the tools to the floor. That quickly got Torsos' attention, but by the time it turned to face me, it was too late. Its mind was mine to play with. I could now look through its head, scramble and distort things. A creature's sight is the easiest to fool. It's the one I always go for first.

This power has a draw back. While inside the mind of another, you have no control over the minds' memories. You would have to live what the other was thinking about while they were trapped. This was useful to find out if a person was deserving to be killed, but sometimes you would be faced with living a traumatic happening in that person's life. An effect that has driven many witches insane.

As I escaped my own mind and into my friend's, I felt something I had never felt before. I had used this spell to take over the minds of many, but this was somehow different. I felt myself fragment, as if water dividing from itself. It was almost as if my friend had two minds. Two individual wills.

As the memories came to focus, I saw darkness, heard the echoing rumble of the Gods, and smelled the familiar scent of blood and old metal.

I was inside a blood soaked container… no… not a container. Where I was felt compact, and comforting to me. Blood all around me.

I could see little light, but enough to recognize the familiar architecture of the room. Brick walls, a steel table. A metal door, likely five inches thick with a single opening covered with bar. It wasn't identical, but very similar to a room I had been in before. This place was much larger, however. But there was something about it that made me feel safe in it.

My friend was peering out of the opening in the door. A room similar to the one he brought me to was outside. Only no pieces of the room lay about, like pieces to a broken puzzle. The walls were whole, the floors were no longer shattered. Everything was neat and orderly. The room was divided by a small flight of steps. The concrete walls and floor were caked in blood and remnants of organs and tissue, but even they seemed to have a place, swept into each sides of the room.

I could feel its body. My friend felt whole... alive, unlike the Torsos I grew to know. I could feel its arms, both the same, and chained to the walls. I could feel it struggling relentlessly trying to free himself, but even as large and strong as it was, it could not move. I could feel its heart beating faster and faster, sinking into its chest. I could hear its screams. The scream of a man—a Stone Walker. Not a beast...

Not Torsos...

I could feel his emotions. Fear, rage, sadness, desperation, hopelessness. Sensations I remember from long ago. They were all there, twisted into a single, intense feeling. The feeling was not the cause of instinct or survival, but from something else. It was confusing me. As hard as I could, I couldn't understand why. I could not describe it.

Most of the room was little more than a blur. My friend was focused on what stood in the center of the room. The silhouette of a man standing at a table, with a light above it, similar to the one I had just been laying on. On the table was a woman, clothes torn from her body, bound by metal and chains. Her screams match that of my friend's. Both intertwined as echoes throughout the crimson walls. However, there was still another sound that could be heard faintly beyond their screams.

The silhouette, seemingly unfazed by their screams, danced about, grabbing a large circular saw from the wall behind him. There was another sound hidden within the screams. A noise I could not recognize. Something I had only heard in populated regions. The crashing and banging of various repetitive noises. The combined noise was something humans seemed to enjoy. A human once told me it was music. Humans have strange names for noise.

The squealing shriek of a saw drowned out their screams. I could feel emotions from my friend that I could not describe or understand as the silhouette approached the young woman wielding a power saw in his hands. A pain in his chest far greater than any pain I have ever felt. The pain became great as the saw touched her flesh. Suddenly, I could feel her pain as well.

First it was her arms. Cut at the shoulder, adding another layer of blood to the floor. I could feel the pain of my lost arm as my friend looked on. I could feel tears falling from his eyes as their screams increased in volume. Then the silhouette cut off her legs. Her screams began to deafen as sporadic gargling took its place. Then nothing. My friend's scream only increased as his eyes leaked more and more.

Finally, he started on the head. I could feel the figure staring at me as he placed the saw blade on her neck. He took his time as the blade began to spin, slowly pushing down onto her flesh. Blood sprayed everywhere, sending crimson droplets spattering against the walls, trickling down them in bizarre, but beautiful, patterns. Her having blood left at all was nothing short of being the product of magic.

Slowly, he pushed the saw into the meat of her throat. Cutting through the jugulars, the windpipe, and the muscles. The sounds of sloshing and gurgling could be heard over the loud scream of the spinning saw. The sound eventually began to quiet, and the blade began to slow as he reached her spine. The saw screeched as it made its way through the bone. Her head fell back, and hung from the thin layer of skin that was still connecting it to the rest of her body.

The shadowed figure took a pair of surgical scissors and snipped the flesh that made the back of her neck. My friend collapsed on himself as the head fell to the floor. His screams turned to whimpers. His tears now added to the floor's various fluids. I could feel every emotion, every tear drop. He fell silent.

The silhouette was now a man, a human, revealed in the light as he walked over to pick up the head of the woman. I couldn't make out any details about him. I could not tell what he truly was, as his face was covered by a mask, wearing a rubber apron over black clothes made crimson with blood. The man stood still, staring at my friend as his mind was lost inside of himself.

The man, the 'Silhouette', raised the head of the woman so both my friend and I could see it. Her head was covered in blood, eyes shut, frozen into a silent rest.

She was beautiful.

Skin pale, nearly white; hair the color of blood. I wasn't sure if that was the color of her hair, or the fact that it was covered in blood.

All I could feel now was rage. Utter, blind rage radiating from my friend. His sadness was gone. All that remained was anger for this shadowed man.

"This is punishment for trying to escape," the Silhouette said behind the head. "I want you to know that this is your fault. This did not have to happen."

"Marvelous creature, isn't she?" The shadowed man went on, lowering her head and cradling it in his hands. He then looked at my friend. "I would have liked

119

to keep her in one piece, but clearly that is no longer a viable option."

He began walking around, moving about the room with the girl's head, seemingly dancing with it.

"The lot of you were perfectly fine where you were," he said, as he waved her head through the air. "But no. You chose freedom over the safety I provided you." He then put his focused back on the giant and I.

"No matter," he whispered. "I have devised… *alternatives.*"

He came back to the cell and raised her head up again. Her eyes were now open and I saw something. Something I had not seen since I was but a small child. I saw something other than the gray, black, and crimson that formed this land. Something other than the blinding white of light. It was a color other than blood red. No, two colors. It's been so long since I have seen them, I've forgotten their names. The two colors danced around her pupils as if looking into an eclipse of the sun.

"What was she to you?" the silhouette asked my friend. "Protector, companion, friend, lover? Perhaps you simply *wished* that to be true." He regarded Torsos for a moment, sighed, and then said, "I have collected enough of you to further my experiment," He walked back to the table which was still occupied by all of her other limbs. "If you wish to be so close to this girl, I will see that you two will remain inseparable."

The memory faded, and a sudden realization came over me, snapping me back into my own mind for a brief moment. Torsos was not just one being. Where I thought I had one friend, I actually had two all this time.

Two bodies and minds joined together in a single form. Molded together using what?

Was it by some human science, or was it the work of a magic that was unknown to me? If it was magic, it must have been very powerful. I had to know. Something that powerful would be useful to have.

This was something to think about later. Right now, Torsos, who I now understand to be two entities, was still in my eyes, even though I was not in theirs. I had control of their eyes now. I had control of what they could and couldn't see now. To them, I was invisible. Torso could not see me as I still lay on the cold metal table. My hand was burning, smoke rising from my palm as I held it out.

That's right, friends. Just keep looking. As long as I did not make a sound, they would think I was gone.

They began searching for me—looking around the room, clearly not knowing what to do. I kept my eyes and hand focused on them. Never blinking, never moving. If I was going to win this game, I needed them to think I had escaped.

Confusion, rage, fear. I could see them all emanating from them. They couldn't find me and as the time passed it only intensified their rage. They began beating the metallic shelves and lockers within the room into bent mutations. With his weapon in hand they left the room, but not before they grabbed my arm, taking it with them.

My arm was tired; it dropped on its own. I fell back on the table, and rolled off. I collapsed onto the floor.

The floor was now a thick black from my own blood. I slowly sat up, lying my back to the table. I could feel fluid slowly run down my cheek. I dabbed the hot liquid with my finger and inspected it. I assumed it to be blood, but the liquid was clear. It quickly dried on my face, and I could feel my eye burn. I was holding my own tear drop in my hand. Not from the pain, or the loss of my limbs, but from Torsos. It was their pain, their loss that caused this phenomena. I had seen tear drops from many, many others. I even held them as I was with my own, but never have I held mine in such a way. Not for a very, very long time.

I wiped the tear between my finger, and looked at the knob that once was my arm. It was odd not seeing it there. The first time I had been parted from my markings since William first etched them on. The blood was slowing down to a low drip, but far from healed. I needed to make some quick repairs to myself before I could continue.

Looking around the room, I found pieces of crimson cloth. One piece should be enough to stop the bleeding. I did my best to tie a knot tightly around what was left of my arm. It didn't stop the blood entirely, but it was enough to keep going.

Now for my leg.

I hopped along, searching the room for a replacement for my missing leg. I found one, a hook, similar to the ones Torsos used to decorate his playground in the corner of the room. A perfect fit. I could tie the loop to what was left of my leg and use the hook as a foot.

After doing what I could to my body, I went about the room collecting my equipment. My wired shirt, my poncho, my pouches and containers, and finally Azathoth and Sothoth, still resting peacefully in their sheaths.

These were my possessions. They are a part of me, just as I am a part of them. They deserve to be a part of me, and no one else. I am sure Torsos understood that. I reattached everything back to my body and reloaded Azathoth's and Sothoth's voices. I was going to need them if I had any chance of getting my arm back.

The Gods were coming back soon. I could feel them. The dust was picking up from the ground. It wouldn't be long before the world around me was nothing but ash and I would be trapped here again until they passed.

My new leg wasn't as good a replacement as I originally thought. I had to obtain a shaft to help support me until I could get back to my old one. The rod I found half buried in the ground among piles of debris, was a useful support once I managed to break it off. I wondered if the grinding and tapping sounds I was making as I carried on through the streets would alert my friends and tell them where I was.

I couldn't climb without all of my limbs, so I was limited to the ground for now. I couldn't even run. I could barely walk. I had seen wounded animals before struggling for survival, but this was the first time I had felt it firsthand. The pain was unfortunately gone, but my body was still weak. I wasn't use to moving so slowly.

I was lucky Torsos didn't think to stop the bleeding once they had me. The blood trail led me right back to my leg. It wasn't far from where they took me, but it still took what seemed like hours to get there.

And there it was, still hanging on the lamp post, right where I left it. Still swaying in the hardening wind, leaking what remained of the blood inside it. The leg was dripping from the severed part as well as a small amount oozing from the hook still lodged into my calf muscle. It was fortunate that my boot and the torn leg of my pants still remained as well. Otherwise, the continually ravenous wind would have damaged it for certain.

I considered how to get it down. The post holding up the chain was too slick to climb, at least not without my arm. I couldn't use Azathoth to shoot the chain either. While the clanging sound of my new leg didn't attract my friends a gunshot surely would, and I wasn't ready for another fight just yet.

I took the rod I had recently acquired and swung it as hard as I could against the post. The rust and age had taken their toll on the post so it was easy to bring it down. It came crashing down with only a few hits. The wires inside were still alive causing the tear to spark with ethereal light. It was blinding even though it was covered by the thick dust.

And there I was, a part of me lying among the

debris. I limped over to my leg as fast as my other would allow, eager to put it back in its place. I sat on the curb and ripped my replacement off, throwing it into the street. I grabbed my leg and held it in my hand examining it.

It was strange seeing what's inside my body. Being able to look at it so clearly—the blackened blood, the grayed, hemorrhaging meat surrounding it. Even the bones were as black as the leather that encased them. The only part of the leg that wasn't black was the skin, which showed almost white in contrast.

As I continued holding... *myself*... in my hand, I thought back to the blood and dismembered bodies I had seen before. I had seen many people's blood before. I had seen humans and giants, witches and Yakshi, Kumuyu, and countless animals. Only The Hidden and I poured black blood from our wounds.

Just as well. Prevented me from trying to see it all

the time.

The smoke poured out the moment I placed my leg back together. It would take a moment to heal completely, but I could walk with it, nonetheless. Getting up, I realized I had not aligned the leg properly—my foot cocked out to the side.

I sighed, and sat back down, pulling my leg back off. The skin stretched and pulled as I forced it off. The nerves had already started reconnecting, so a lot of force was needed to pull the leg back apart. I grunted and heaved as the small layer of skin ripped, and the tendons stretched and snapped.

After a little work, and a small amount of pain, I managed to get it off so that I could line the bones up and place it right. I stood up to make sure, testing the alignment, bending my knee to make sure of its usefulness. It felt right. Nothing stuck out, and the bone didn't give way.

I had what I needed to repair my clothes, but that took time. Time that I wanted to get my arm back and say hello to Torsos again. For now the disconnected leg of my pants flopped over my boot, revealing my knee, and scar where it was severed. I could patch it another time. Finding small things like patching equipment helped prevent boredom when I was trying to pass the time. For now I already had other things to do.

12

It was time to find my friends. The Stone Walker, the Lady Arm, and William the Knife. It was ironic Torsos had him *and* my arm. After all, he repaired my markings for me. And Azathoth and Sothoth barely got to know him before Torsos took him from us. I would have to be sure to take him back when we met again.

I knew where I might find them, though, I wasn't sure if it really was the place I thought they would be, or if I just wanted to visit it again. The garden of bodies was where I wanted to go. I wanted to see the decorations again. I wanted to see the hollowed torsos and perhaps see my friends while I was there.

The wind was getting louder, making it easier to move about without detection. I took my time, walking on the ground instead of climbing the artificial lands. I was ready to witness the field again, but I was in no hurry. With the wind as it was, I would surely hear my friends before they heard me.

I could start to smell the rotting flesh. I was near the field. I let the scent grace my nostrils as the rest of my senses hungered for more. My eyes wanted to see, my skin wanted to touch. Even my tongue salivated for a taste. The closer I got, the stronger my senses hungered. The more I anticipated getting there.

And as the dust unveiled them, there they were. hanging in the streets against the pillars and walls of the artificial land. The field had been bigger than I remembered, as the more I went on, the more I saw. The headless, limbless bodies. All designed differently and uniquely, but all with the same similarities.

Like a family.

My eyes seemed thrilled as they darted from one to the other until they stopped at one on the ground, chained to a fence made of stone and blackened steel pikes. I knelt down, appreciating the art as I touched it with the tip of my fingers. The body was male, thin, and scarred. Much like me.

I thought of how close I was to becoming a part of this family. I thought about how disappointed I was that I was not. If I had, I would not be able to appreciate these wonders as I do. I wouldn't be able to gaze upon the rest of them as I am now. I think I prefer it this way.

My eyes turned their gaze upon what laid behind the fence. A field that seemed nearly untouched by the Gods. The grass, while dead, still remained. The wind had not uprooted it yet. The field was surrounded on all sides by large structures. Or it would be better to say it was one big building that surrounded this place. Seems not even the Gods liked to come here. It was filled with artificial stones humans used to mark their dead. It was a graveyard. I've seen many in my journeys, but this one was spectacular. Almost breathtaking, for not only were there bodies underneath, they were above as well.

There were nearly a hundred of them just within this small field. The bodies were extensively decomposed here. The scent of rot almost had a physical presence here—strong enough to touch with your hands. It was like a garden of decomposed torsos, far more here than anywhere else in this dead city. This is where it started. This was where Torsos began their playground.

I wanted to take my time and absorb the sights. From the center I could see the entire field. Bodies chained to the walls, impaled on the gates, like everywhere else but this was better as even dead stones were used to display them. It was like experiencing an emotion. As if I could hear the screams from these vessels.

And then I saw it. Blackness in the dust. At first, I thought it was Torsos, but the size and shape wasn't right. Though it was hard to tell in the dust, this was not a blackness caused by an object, but the lack of one. It was a hole. A large hole in the side of one of the buildings. For some reason I felt an attraction to it. A connection, even. My curiosity was screaming at me.

I wanted to know what was there.

The closer I got to it, the more my attraction increased. As if pulling me in. I couldn't stop myself even if I wanted to. The metal and concrete that once made a wall were scatter and broken from the outside. As if something broke out from the inside.

Standing just outside the hole looking in, I could see nothing, but the blackness. As if there was nothing in there at all, but void. My naked eyes were useless. The blackness was too thick. Was there a floor? Was there anything? My mark of fire was on my arm. I had no light I could simply conjure. I would have to make do.

My first step revealed the floor to me. It was concrete by the sound of it; broken, and covered in ash, leading downward into more blackness. The echoes from my second step revealed the walls. Broken like the floor, and spread far apart, but increasingly closer as the descending floor continued on.

My third step revealed a flight of steps. Stone, covered in more dust and rock. As I descended the steps, I could see how they looked by my ears and feet. These steps were broken—cracked—divided like the earth they were built upon, but still held solid. The bottom lead to a large platform made of the same material as the steps that lead to another flight. Then another, then another. The steps were repeating themselves as I descended further into the darkness.

My eyes started to adjust to the dark as I made my way down. The path became more restricting as the steps finally came to an end. The floor became smoother, but no less dust covered it. The floors and walls now resembled that of a normal hallway. Doors that bent from the outside filled the hallway in parallel intervals. The doors were so heavy and damaged, it was impossible to open them.

The blackness faded as I continued. At the end was another opening—an opening that beckoned me. It felt like this was the place that was pulling me further in. I was drawn to it, like an insect to light. It called to me. I could almost hear it calling out to me, whispering to me in a soft voice to come closer.

My eyes were adjusted enough, but the room inside the opening was still far too black to see anything. Even the floor and walls felt different: the scent, the feel, the aura. The room felt familiar, comforting.

I felt at ease there. I felt at home.

As I entered, I walked around in the blackness, unable to make anything out. I assumed I was in a void until I felt another set of steps on the floor. Unable to see them, I just guessed where the next was as I made my way up. The steps were not long like those I had just descended. No, there were only four steps before reaching the last one. The final step, though, wasn't a step at all. It gave way as I lay my foot on it, making a loud click. Another trap, I thought at first, but then a light came on in front of me.

I was blinded by the light at first. I shielded my eyes with my hand. As my eyes focused. I looked down at the blood-covered ground to see what my foot was on. It was a small metal thing. Small pieces of steel rods connected to a spring-operated paddle. A wire, which led into the blackness (and likely the walls), was sticking out of the back of it. I looked up at the light again to see

140

what else the light revealed and suddenly a blood-soaked table stood before me.

The table was made of steel, like the one Torsos had me on. Only this one was much older. The blood on it had dried years ago, as well as the blood around it. A lot of people had died here. This table somehow seemed familiar. Not that I had been on a similar one, but as if I've seen this very same table before.

The room around the light was still black, but I could now see why. Just outside the light I could see a familiar sight. Black smoke and the faint, familiar scent of magic. Like tentacles reaching out to take the light. The smoke was dancing around me, as if it was attracted to me. I inhaled it as more gathered around me, absorbing it into my lungs.

I looked back down at the device that operated the light. It was strange to see such a thing here, and it still have power and function. What purpose could this have? To allow your feet to control the light? Its odd reasoning sparked my curiosity. Why are you here little thing? What's your purpose? I wondered if the light would turn back off if I struck it with my foot again.

The lights did not turn off. No, just the opposite. Light now surrounded me. The entire room was now lit as I struck for a second time. I saw the blood-stained power tools to my left. The barred rooms, the chains, the hooks. This was the room where the woman was butchered. This was the place I saw through the giant's eyes.

The room where Torsos was born.

The walls were covered in etchings written in Wiccan. The words were still speaking to me. Smoke was still radiating from them, like a flame trying to escape through the cracks of the walls. It was mesmerizing.

Unexpected. Confusing.

What confused me the most was the fact that the

spells remained alive. This told me two things. That the spells were written in the blood of a witch, and that witch was still alive. These spells, this blood, would not have beckoned to me if it had been otherwise.

The power within our blood dies the moment we die. Whoever wrote these spells or at least whose ever blood this was, was surely still living. Still out there with all the answers to my questions. What did these messages mean? What did they do? Who were they? If they were powerful enough to create Torsos...

To put two minds into the same body, who knows what other kinds of spells this Witch may know.

A Witch.

A witch so powerful and deadly that it could put two minds into one body. This is the reason why the other creatures of this world fear us. It's why they hate us. We bastardize their world to make it our own. To overcome the things that hinder them the most. Our language does not speak to them as it does to us.

As it does to the world.

I looked at them all. Every last spell printed on the walls.

Hours may have gone by by the time I stopped. Some I

recognized, but most were unfamiliar. The state of their

decay showed me that this room had been abandoned for

years. It was clear that if it had been that Silhouette who

wrote these, he had long since abandoned this place.

I wanted to mark these spells into my flesh, but

doing so without knowing their potential could prove

fatal. Looking around the room, I found pieces of leather.

I laid the leather on the table, stuck my finger into what

was left of my right arm. Using my own blood, I copied as many of them as could fit onto the leather, making sure to perfectly match every curve, every line, every symbol.

The leather was completely filled from one side, to the other. From front to back. And with it written in my own blood, I could control whether or not the spells came alive. They would not respond to me unless I wanted them to.

As much as the room comforted me, as much as I didn't want to leave, there was nothing there for me— nothing but the messages. My priority was to find my arm and likely find my friends in the process. It was time to go and get back what's mine.

I made my way back up the stairs. This time it was far easier to find them. As dark as the outside was, the contrast to the hall still made the exit clearly visible. It was a light at the end of the tunnel only when lightning struck nearby. The flashes briefly blinding me each time, but it lit my path well enough for me to see it.

Outside, the wind was picking up. The black wires and chains above were swinging about sporadically, and my poncho was moving about with a mind of its own. It wouldn't be long before the Gods returned and reclaimed their lands. It seemed I was going to be here when they did.

I let the wind caress my face as I stood in the dead grass. It felt good. Like the embracing touch of a woman with cold hands. I stood in place feeling the wind for a while, wondering what I should do. I had no clues what direction Torsos might be in. I figured that I could just wait. I felt they would come back eventually. Though I didn't have to wait long as I heard an all too familiar sound.

Metal scratching the asphalt. A noise similar to the screeches of a dying Lurker. A sound so loud, it practically shook the ground.

Scratch… scratch… scratch…

Every slow, long scrape got louder and louder.

Until…

There they were.

They were in my sight. Torsos. dragging the immense weapon against the ground. But in *her* hand was my arm, holding me delicately and tenderly by the hand. I got the feeling she enjoyed holding it.

It was still dripping blood.

Drip… drip… drip…

A trail of black blood drops followed them with every step they made. My arm looked to be well taken care of, which was surprising. Their first reaction to seeing it was dictated by fear and hate. I expected to see it mangled, skinned, destroyed. But there it was, completely intact.

I was glad they took care of it. Perhaps she

protected it from him. Maybe she knew I wanted it back. Maybe she knew I needed it. Maybe she wanted to die and I needed it to kill them. The question was: would she give it willingly? I appreciated her looking after it, but I needed it back.

What was the best way to get it? Trying to take it would end in my being crushed. No, that wouldn't do. Torsos was just far too fast and powerful for me to just take it. No, I needed them to get close to me and trap them. If I could get them stuck, I could take it back with little difficulty.

I will admit, it was nice to see them. The Stone Walker, Lady Arm, and William the Knife calmly sitting in their chest. I instinctively put on a mask for them. The curl of my lips, and rear of my teeth. A smile. Though they probably couldn't see it, I still did so anyway.

"Friends," I said without even noticing.

Suddenly the stone was again agile. Fast,

inhumanly so. I could hear the wind break as Torsos violently swung the weapon, sending it flying towards me. It ravenously tore through the air, spinning so fast, my eyes couldn't process it all.

Dodging it wasn't hard. In fact, I didn't have to dodge it at all. I only had to move my head just slightly. Only the wind from its force struck me. I could hear the increasing sound of the whirl as it passed by me.

The crash from the violent weapon was loud and poured enough dust in the wind to slightly cloud my vision. The chain of the weapon was there beside me, stretched out in the air between Torsos and the weapon, which was now lodged in the wall behind me. This chain was a nuisance. Many times it has gotten in my way. It was time to do away with it.

I pulled Azathoth out, and took aim. I fired a single shot into the chain and broke it in two. The chain hit the ground as the tension gave way. I was glad to finally be rid of it, but I'm sure my friends did not share the same sentiment.

It was clear Torsos was not happy with my decision to break his beloved weapon. They set into my direction, smashing into everything that stood between me and them. The dead mounts in the streets, the gate in the field, the tombstones. Nothing slowed them down to get to me.

I didn't have long to decide what I was going to do. Torsos is big, heavy, and turns slowly. I am small, light, and agile. I'd have to use that as my advantage. Take the strength coming at me, and use it against my opposing force. Torsos was on me quickly. I could feel even the wind getting out of their way. With its right arm arched back ready to rip me apart, it was time to make a move, and quickly, or risk being merged with the ground.

I leaped into the air and grabbed Torsos by the shoulder as the arm plowed the earth beneath me.

I flipped over them and landed behind them. While crouched, I took aim with Azathoth, and fired a shot into their back.

The shot did nothing but piss off the Stone Walker even more. They took a swing at me, but they're not the only one with speed on their side. Being this close, I could stay to their back. Staying behind made things easier, but staying there was difficult. It was hard to stay silent as well, and at this range, they both could clearly see me. Remembering that, I had to remember to keep a smile.

How do I penetrate this thing's flesh? Shots from Azathoth just bounce off and I was low of rounds for Sothoth. If I had my arm, I could rely on a couple of my spells. I needed it back, but while it was in Torsos' possession, it was near impossible to get it.

I continued thinking, deciding what to do as Torsos continued to take swipes at me.

What to do?

I rattled my brain until I saw it, and it finally dawned on me. The answer was obvious. While most of Torsos was made of nearly impenetrable flesh, there was one part that was not—

Her.

I dodged out of yet another violent swing, and took aim at the soft, flesh of the woman's arm.

I hesitated.

"Sorry," I whispered before I pulled the trigger on Azathoth.

The bullet pierced right through her arm. She dropped my hand to the ground. I rolled for it as the Stone Walker continued his wild attacks. I grabbed my arm and quickly darted towards a mass of tombstones.

It was in my hand. Finally. I hadn't realized that her arm was still clamped onto mine. I tried to pull hers away from mine by tucking mine under my other arm and yanking on hers. After some effort, she finally released her grip. She must have been fond of it. Maybe she had grown an attachment to the markings.

I was almost whole again. I sat on the dirt, hiding behind the gravestones. I unwrapped the stub and placed my arm back in its rightful place. I held it there, snapping the bones into place and making sure everything was right as the healing took effect. My entire arm puffed up in black smoke as I could feel the skin fuse together. I was finally whole again.

Well, almost whole.

I felt something moving on the ground. The woman's arm was still grasping around, trying to grab a hold of something. I assumed when I removed it from the giant, she would die. I pick up the arm and held her in my hand. Her muscles twitching, her finger reaching out as if desperately trying to grab on to me. I felt a bond with her. Discarding her seemed wrong. I couldn't just leave her. I took her and let her grab my shoulder blade as I stood up. She latched onto my poncho and hung from my back.

I peeked out from the headstones trying to get an idea of what Torsos, or at least what was left of him, was doing. I could hear the loud, indescribable whaling as he rampaged through the graves. Either he was looking for me, or just raging from the loss of her arm. I may have hit a nerve stealing her away.

That's fine. Just go ahead and rage for a bit, my friend. While you're at it, I'm gonna wait for my arm to heal and figure out how I want to strike. Even though I have my arm back, I'm still going to kill you. It's the least I can do for you.

I watched and waited, wondering if there was a fast and easy way to kill him. Most of his flesh was rock hard, but he'll still bleed if I penetrate it. I would like it if he bled for me. I'm curious to see what the inside of him looks like. Who knows how much he has been mutilated on the inside. It might be interesting to see.

I watched and waited for just the right time.

And there it was.

His back was to me. This was my chance to attack. I leaped from headstone to headstone, and dashed towards the giant. He would hear me, but if I was fast enough, he would not have time to react.

My feet took to the air as I got closer. I flew through the wind, and latched onto his back, and griped onto his shoulder as I pulled Azathoth from her holster and fired what remained of her bullets into Torsos' back.

As I held on, Torsos tried to sling me off, struggling to knock me from his back. It was fun. Jerking me about, ramming into graves, doing everything he could to get me off of him. My legs flung through the air uncontrollably. There were times he came close to throwing me off, but my grip was strong and locked in place.

While I was on this mountain of rock and meat, I took the time to inspect his flesh. To see if there were any weak points. The bullets I fired only chipped away at his stone flesh. Not doing much to get at his gelatinous insides. But like any rock, there had to be cracks, gaps, anything in between the muscles that I could exploit.

I wanted to see it; I *craved* seeing his blood.

Nothing would stop me from seeing it, from feeling it. That had been on my mind since I first laid eyes on this creature. He is my prey and I will not stop until my prey is dead and his insides are his outsides.

Shooting his back was useless. There was no point wasting bullets trying to pierce through. It would take far more ammo than I had to make my way into him. But there was one place that I had already pierced him. Where I had jabbed William into him. Right there. It was the closest chance I had to get to his guts and finally do some damage to him.

He threw himself into a wall. The force jerked me forward. I wasn't ready to release him yet. Not after I had my prey so close. I latched onto William's handle. There I was, hanging onto William, dangling off of Torsos' front. My feet dangled from his body. I was vulnerable at this point. He could easily kill me now.

He grabbed onto my legs with his one arm. He yanked me from him, and William went with me. He slammed me into the ground before picking me back up by my leg. He raised me up, legs first, until we were face to face. I was reminded of hanging from the hook before I lost my leg. He was looking at me, like a curious animal. Did he still want to kill me? What was he waiting for? Maybe he thought I already was. The impact rattled my body quite a bit.

I took his moment of curiosity as a time to survive. I reached my right arm out and set fire to his head. The shock and surprise caused him to sling me away. I hit the fence and the metal bars folded like wet paper. I landed and rolled into the road. Injured, but still able, my body reluctantly brought itself back to its knees. William was still in my hand. I looked down at him.

"Hello, old friend. It's been some time."
I threw him up in the air and caught him before sliding him into my boot. It was only then I realized I had gained one friend, and lost another. My arm friend was was no longer attached to me. She was probably detached when Torsos flung me.

I didn't have time to look for her. Torsos wasn't done with me. There he was, lurking outside of the gate, suddenly hurdling towards me, like a natural disaster. Before I knew it, he was upon me, ready to tear me apart. My head was encased by his giant hand. I quickly pulled at his wrist, pounding on it with all of my strength. If bullets couldn't do anything to his flesh, there was little my bare hands could.

He picked me up the air and slammed my body into the asphalt. I went limp as he picked me up again. And again he slammed me into the asphalt. This time I could feel the rocky ground give way underneath me. My head started to bleed. I could feel the pressure as Torsos tightened his grip around my skull. I only had one eye that wasn't covered by his flesh. I used that eye to look into his before he could crush me.

Everything slowed down. I looked into his eyes for what seemed like hours. I looked into his gray, dead eyes. I recognized those eyes—the eyes of a soulless creature. A creature that is only driven by instinct. I've seen those eyes before.

This creature, the Torsos is just like *me*.

As I stared at my friend, my kindred friend, I could feel myself beginning to black out. My eyes began to close, my body began to give way. I could feel my blood covering my face. Soon it was all I could see, but just for one moment, I thought I felt something… Blood. Just blood…

Drip…

Drip….

Wait. The blood was dripping onto me. Why would my blood be dripping on me? Where was it coming from? The blood spilling on me forced me to open my eye again. And then I saw it. I could see the color of crimson once again instead of black. The blood was coming from the wound William called home just moments ago.

There it was. I finally got to see Torsos bleed. But this was my chance to kill him. I quickly reached for Sothoth and took aim. I promised I'd kill you, and I aim to keep that promise.

"Goodbye, friend," I said to him in a whisper.

I pulled the trigger.

The round went into his wound and pierced straight through. I was hoping the bullet would stay inside him. Turn Torsos into an empty shell. But instead, the bullet came out of his back, and into the building above. I wasn't sure if it was enough to kill him. I did feel his grip loosen, but there was still life in him. If it wasn't enough if would be the end of me.

I had no more rounds left inside Sothoth. Oh well. Seems like a suitable way to die. I wonder if my new friends will miss me once I'm gone.

I could feel the explosion above me. I could hear it, but I could not see it. Torsos' massive body shielded my vision. It must have been a massive explosion as even the ground shook as Sothoth's hand sang. Sothoth has a loud voice, but not as loud as what I was hearing. I could see rubble falling on either side of Torsos. Rumbling began to fall on either side of me. I could hear the sound of moving rock and steel. Part of the building was coming down.

As pieces of debris were falling around Torsos, I was still trapped in his grip. The crashing rock wasn't enough to get his attention either. He was fully focused on me. If he didn't kill me soon, the debris would kill us both. I'd rather die by his hand than be smashed by pieces of a building.

I could finally see it coming down: a large piece of concrete, a stone pillar coming right for us. I was blacking out, the sound of the pillar was deafening. Looks like we'd be dying together after all. Just as well. Two animals of the same breed meeting their end together.

It felt right.

Then it all went black.

I was awakened by a hard thud against my shoulder. I felt it, but I did not bother to see what it was. I wasn't sure if I was in one piece or not. I wasn't even sure if I was alive. All of my senses were gone. I was numb, my ears were deaf, my breath was gone, I could not see. For all I knew I could have been dead. Death was a new experience for me. How was I supposed to know how it felt?

My vision finally started to come back to me. Dust, blood, and rock all swimming together in a giant blur was all I could see, but I could still see nonetheless. My breath finally came back to me, I could smell and taste once again. Pain came back to my body. I still could not hear, but I knew I wasn't dead yet.

The first thing I saw when I wiped the blood from my eyes was the giant. As still and lifeless as the city itself. His grip was loosened enough to get free, but I still laid their underneath him for a while, looking into those dead eyes. They were always lifeless but they looked even more familiar now.

I looked over to my right to see what was on my shoulder. Seemed my arm friend managed to find me again.

"Hey," I said to her with an empty smile.

I finally pulled my head out, and rolled out from under him. I inspected my new environment. First thing that was apparent was that I was still in one piece. All of my limbs were still attached and it seemed my arm friend was unharmed as well. Huge chunks of of the building behind was in the street. When I looked, I saw the large hole in the side of it, exposing many of the higher floors. The most notable change was all the blood. This massive giant that just died for me had a lot of it to spill.

Rock and metal, even the wind seemed red now with Torsos' blood. It was almost as if the debris, itself was bleeding. It was hard to tell what was rubble and what was Torsos'. The pillar had crushed his legs almost completely. Rock and metal piercing his back, rubble lay on the ground all over him, but one place.

Underneath him.

Torsos had saved me.

The force of the falling pillar had completely ripped Torsos entire bottom half from the rest of him. Only a small stretch of one of his legs and his massive feet were still exposed. His head was mostly smashed in. His blood lay all over the surrounding rock. My friend was finally dead, or so I thought.

His arm began to slowly move. It was surprising

and impressive how much Torsos refused to give up.

Despite being in such disrepair, he was still trying to come at me, slowly crawling with his one arm. As he slowly made his way to me, I just watched. This giant, this *thing*, was almost pitiful. He reached out to me. I reached out to him. My fingertips touched his hand before he finally collapscd.

My friend was no more.

I continued looking at him even after his death. I looked at him, contemplating things through. He looks familiar crushed to pieces like that. He almost looks like a real torso now. I think I know what my friend would like for me to do.

It took some time and a lot of force, but using a few chains and the remnants from a dead mount, I was finally able to get my friend back to the garden. I couldn't carry him down to the garden that he had created, so I had to make do with what I could get to cut him apart.

After all of the damage he took from the rubble, it was relatively easy to prepare him. His head just seemed to come off after a few hard whacks with William. There was little of him left, but the arm was just far too thick to cut.

After touching up the body with a couple of chains hooked into his flesh, I hoisted him to a pulley I made on the center of the top floor of the building that lead to the place he was born. It took nearly all of my strength to finally get him lifted up to where I wanted him, but I hooked the chains into the building so he wouldn't go anywhere.

Once done, I climbed back down and took a look at what I had accomplished. There he was. In the middle of the world he had created, surrounded by his works of art...

His family.

And there he was at the top point to keep watch

over them. I stood there staring at his torso, proud of what I had done. I think my friend would approve. I was a little disappointed it was over already. It's been a long time since I had so much fun. At least I have the memories.

As I studied the torso one last time, I could see something moving inside him. The flesh around the wound where I shot him was beginning to break apart, making the wound even bigger and exposing an organ. The organ hung from him until finally giving way and falling to the ground.

I approached this massive blob of meat and blood after it had stopped rolling on the ground. What was it? Was this his heart? Too small to be a heart of a giant. What the Hell was it? Perhaps this was a keepsake for me. I picked the organ up and pulled the guts off…

Hair, eyes, nose, mouth… teeth…

It was a head.

Long hair, small chin, feminine features. This was

the head of a woman. The more I cleaned off of her, the more details I could make out. She was beautiful. The head had been violently severed, but the expression on her face was peaceful. She looked familiar. Was this the woman? Was this the second mind I felt inside Torso? Was this my other friend?

I remembered her eyes. Those two colors swirling together. If the eyes were the same, there would be no mistaking who this was. I pulled one of her eye lids open, and there they were. Not like the colors I saw in Torsos' mind, but I could see the two shades that danced around her pupil. I then felt a delicate tug on my shoulder. I looked back and felt my arm friend tighten her grip.

It was then I realized I needed to smile.

Hey.

Who *are* you?

The saga continues in

THE CRIMSON GIRL

Coming soon in the
BLACKHEARTS
series

Made in the USA
Lexington, KY
12 May 2016